a novella

by Eirik Gumeny

AtomicCarnivalBooks.com

Albuquerque, New Mexico

INFERNAL ORGANS

Atomic Carnival Books
Albuquerque, N.M.

First Edition

ISBN 979-8-9884520-4-1

Cover and book design by Eirik Gumeny

This book is a work of fiction. Names, characters, places, brands, and events are either the product of the author's imagination or used fictitiously. Any resemblance to actual persons, places, incidents, monsters, and organs, living, dead, or otherwise, is entirely coincidental.

also from
ATOMIC CARNIVAL
BOOKS

OPEN ALL NIGHT
an anthology of retail horror

GREATER THAN HIS NATURE
thrilling tales of mad science

EAT THE RICH
an anthology of carnivorous anti-capitalism

for everyone
who's lost a little of
themselves

and has a little
of someone else
instead

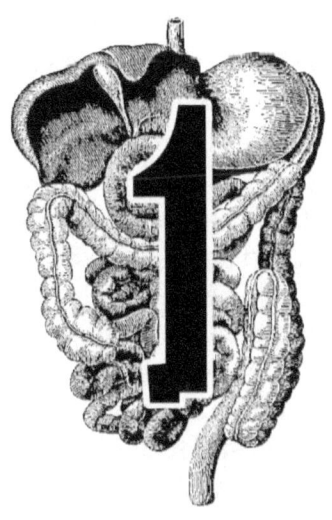

THE DINGHY SETTLED ALONG THE MUDDY SHORE, drifting softly into the cutout between the marsh grass. The old boat, soft and splintering wood and peeling paint, rocked and creaked as the passenger stepped from within, as she dragged it farther up the mire, free from the lapping tide.

The woman was young, no more than thirty, wearing a Baja hoodie, an oversized wool pullover, popular among hippies and other assorted stoners, red and black and baggy over her small yet robust frame. Shoulder-length brown hair was pulled back messily, out of her face, but not much more. Her skin was soft and brown, glowing warm in the dying light of the day. She grabbed a worn canvas messenger bag from inside the boat and slipped the strap over her head.

Slats of warped palmetto, a half-forgotten board-walk, led her through swampy stalks, over runnels of seawater, toward Ingolstadt proper. Battered fenceposts shivered along the edges of the onetime resort, beach and marsh giving way to the unkempt grass of the small island. A dozen cottage houses, slumping into the soft earth, formed a nearly-complete circle surrounding Grimke Manor, the estate sitting atop a small hill like a ramshackle crown, gilt and guttered at once.

The mansion, laid out like a pixelated circle, seemed to face all sides simultaneously—there was no clear front, too many doors, too many corners—an all-seeing Janus of a building. Its roof, steeply angled and broadly flat at intervals, was lined with stabbing spines of iron; gabled windows jut out like busted teeth. A trio of rounded towers rose at uneven interludes. Against the deepening gray of the sky, the charcoal trim and bricks of weathered crimson nearly swallowed, the manor felt ethereal and half-seen, a bad dream.

A chill ran through Eliza Duran then, a creep that crawled up the whole of her back, accompanied by one thought, and one thought only.

She really wished she'd worn warmer pants.

Once upon a time—always, upon a lot of times, actually—Eliza would have been described as being too smart for her own good. There hadn't been a single moment of her childhood when she hadn't been reading, getting into trouble, or reading something that was going to get her into trouble. She was always taking things apart and putting them back together again, asking people too many questions, even as they yelled at her for disassembling their watches while they weren't looking. She'd graduated high school at sixteen, college before she was twenty, got a master's in civil engineering followed by one in biotechnology. She'd literally grown a bridge once, a prototype, used it as a bookshelf and held up an entire set of research encyclopedias. Her brain was, conservatively, the size of a planet.

And yet here she was, DoorDashing pot for a living.

Here she was, forgetting to check the goddamn weather, to look at her goddamn phone for more than two goddamn seconds before hopping into a rickety-ass rowboat and hauling two pounds of Egon's World into the cold winds of a *clearly* fronting storm, while wearing Tevas, hiking sandals, and torn-up jeans when her boots and fleece-lined cargos had been *right there.*

At least Viktoriya Hong was the kind of eccentric who tipped well.

Readjusting the bag over her shoulder, Eliza followed the trail of palm boards up the hill, toward the misshapen mansion, the chimera of architecture—the place was an almost textbook example of a Queen Anne, only maybe two or three of them at once, with hints of Second Empire and Hayao Miyazaki to boot—trying to remember on which door on what side she was supposed to knock. She was coming up from the south, some old smuggler's path from Prohibition or the Age of Pirates, or at least that's what she told herself. The main dock, the real one, was to the west. Cannabis was still *super* illegal in South Carolina, even this far into the future, into 20fucking23, so the least she could do was play the role.

She'd always wanted to be Han Solo anyway.

It wasn't until Eliza got closer to Grimke Manor, until the walls began to loom and the mansion's shadow fell over her, that she saw the fence. The barricade. Cobbled together from scraps and strips and wooden boards, covered in broken glass and barbed wire like something out of *Fortnite*, and lashed to the posts of the wraparound porch with unlit Christmas lights. It had to be at least six-feet tall, continuing around the house, no gaps, not even small ones.

That's when she heard the quiet, too—when she *felt* it, more than anything—sudden and intense. The gentle swash of the tide had receded, the wind weakened to less than a whisper. There were no people, no birds, no frogs.

There were always frogs.

Then, in the tall grass to her right, a noise. An almost silent rustling, like the shuffling of paper, that rang out like a gunshot. Her body tensed instinctively, and then, upon recognizing the sound as the movement of something small crawling and crunching through a half-dead winter lawn, relaxed almost as quickly.

There *were* frogs, after all. She was just being paranoid.

Thank the bouncing baby Christ, she thought. *This is why you don't get high before a delivery, Eliza.*

The something small continued toward her, inch by inch. The grass trembling as it moved closer, carving the tiniest trail of indent and shadow.

Eliza smiled and leaned down, hands clasped, elbows on thighs.

"Hey, Mr. Frog," she said, "you gave me quite the scare there, little buddy."

The quivering grass paused, as if hearing her, understanding her, before redoubling its pace and closing the distance. The something small finally came into view. Not a frog, Eliza saw, but a snake. She could have done without snakes, but at least—

No.

Snakes didn't look like that.

Snakes weren't segmented like giant worms.

Snakes weren't the dull pink of internal organs.

This wasn't a snake.

This was a large intestine.

This was a large fucking intestine.

And it was holding a crowbar.

"What in the actual f—"

The intestine lunged, squeezing and springing, spearing the jagged end of the rusted crowbar at Eliza's face. She tumbled backwards, narrowly avoiding being skewered, and watched the choleric colon, wriggling and emitting a gurgling hiss, sail over her, landing in the grass on the other side.

Scrambling, Eliza started up the path toward the house, the rampart of danger-trash. A sudden, pressing need to be on the other side of it seized her; she'd climb the damn thing if she had to, bleeding hands be damned.

Unfortunately, it seemed that the large intestine— given the farting slithers she could hear behind her, the dull and drumming thud of metal dragged on wood—had the same idea.

"Eliza!"

She looked up. A man she didn't recognize was holding a hatch in the fence open, was ushering her inside. His dark eyes were darting across the grass, the island, everywhere but at her.

Eliza didn't keep him waiting.

THE INSIDE OF GRIMKE MANOR WAS DIFFERENT than Eliza had been expecting. Ingolstadt, she knew, had been a resort on-and-off over the years, starting in the 1800s when leisure was first invented, and was currently a rental property, the kind you could find on VRBO and Airbnb and the like. One of those aspirationally swanky places everyone knew *about*, a little, but nobody ever actually went to; Eliza had seen it advertised to her on Instagram on occasion. There was even a ritzy ferry service available—to richer and more patient visitors than her anyway.

All of which was to say: Eliza expected *something* to be updated, modernized, brought into some part of the last century. Instead, standing in the massive foyer, it was like she'd stepped back into the Gilded Age. Gold touches and extravagant molding etched the walls like ornate jewelry; saffron wallpaper, with floral designs more intricate than some blueprints she'd seen, covered everything else. The floor was a single slab of polished marble; the ceiling was sectioned in wood and tin. Enormous windows were blanked by lush, emerald drapes, thick and soft enough that a person could probably sleep in them. A beautifully complicated table, adorned with an equally overwrought lamp, both of which looked like they'd been borrowed from the Smithsonian, sat in the center of the entrance hall. Twin staircases curved upward on either side, twisting like DNA strands.

And that, Eliza couldn't help but note, was just *this* room.

"Eliza, hello," said the mysterious man from moments earlier, turning from the triple-locked door and holding out his hand. He was older, well-dressed, almost annoyingly handsome: sharp jaw, dimpled chin, piercing brown eyes, impossibly smooth olive skin. His thick, graying hair was pulled back tightly, into a short ponytail that managed to project refinement instead of *let me tell you a story about Woodstock*-ment. A silver fox and tall, dark, and handsome combined into one, the wet dream of a romance author.

"I'm Clement."

She shook his hand.

"Clement Henry," he continued, with a voice so mellifluous Eliza wondered if maybe she was a romance author, too. His hands were calloused, sure as stone, yet warm and soft—hard work and vanity simultaneously. "Viktoriya and I are working on a project together, a thesis of hers upon which we're trying to expound."

Eliza couldn't place his accent. English, but not quite.

"Please," Clement said, gesturing to his left, "if you could make your way into the parlor. Viktoriya has been waiting for you. I can fetch you some tea? Coffee?"

"Coffee would be great," Eliza answered. Then: "Are

we just not gonna talk about the large intestine that tried to Tonya Harding's husband's friend my face?"

"All in good time, my dear."

"And 'good time' is … how long exactly?"

"About as long as it takes to brew a pot of coffee."

"Yeah, all right," she grumbled in agreement.

Eliza started toward the other room, this one done up in burgundy between all the gold—the parlor, apparently, something she'd thought went out of style with the dinosaurs—passing through an arch that clearly belonged in a fancy French park somewhere. In the corner, jarringly jolly, was a garishly-appointed Christmas tree, lit with at least three different kinds of colored lights.

Viktoriya Hong was sitting on a large sofa, noticeably worse for wear. Not unwell, necessarily, but run-down. Haggard, as if she'd been awake for days. Her black hair was wild and knotted, which wasn't itself new, but it was down and falling in her face rather than pulled back. Her fair skin blotchy where it wasn't pallid. Her eyes, too, weren't hinting red but genuinely bloodshot, with dark bags underneath. Her flowing, Stevie Nicks-esque garb was buried beneath an oversized cardigan, exacerbating her thin frame. And she was more still than Eliza had ever seen the whirlwind of a woman before. Tea cups and soup bowls, fine china all, cluttered the coffee table.

"Hello, Elizabeth," she said, smiling.

"Hey, Vik," Eliza replied, sitting down beside her and flipping open her messenger bag. "I brought your weed, if you—" She paused. "Are you okay?"

"Oh, fine, fine. Just a little tired."

"You sure?"

"Oh, yes. Clement has been taking excellent care of me. We had a bit of a scare the other day, that's all. Everything's all right now. Just takes a little longer to recuperate at my age, but you know that."

"It's not your heart?"

"For once, no." She shot Clement, entering the room with coffee and cookies, a look. "*My* heart isn't the problem."

Eliza's eyebrow arched.

So this was more than just a business arrangement.

That would explain a lot actually.

This place, this mansion, didn't seem like Vik at all. She was a crunchy granola-type, low maintenance and lower effort. Wearing the same clothes since the sixties, spending the better part of two decades living in a yurt, a questionably cult-y commune, dreaming up ways to solve world hunger or save the bees or train raccoons to steal back stolen art. She had a thousand ideas and chased all of them, and, as a result, never really got anything done. That was something they had in common, actually. Big and gaudy and isolated—forced to focus on one thing—really wasn't Vik's style.

Viktoriya and Eliza had met four years ago, while Eliza was TaskRabbiting—after she'd lost her job, but before she'd lost all hope. She'd been putting up Christmas lights and assembling IKEA furniture in garages, anything she could do without having to go inside someone's house. Vik had needed her help re-locating the Airstream in which she'd been living, after the owner of the property she'd been camping on proved unmoved by her pleas of elder abuse and squatters' rights and interrupting the scientific process.

Towing a trailer and the accompanying string of volatile stills was certainly more than Eliza had been expecting, but she had a truck, and she wasn't going to turn down good money. And when Vik, sitting beside her in the cab, didn't flinch as she slid an N95 over her ears, and, in fact, as Vik herself pulled a mask from her pocket—something about as common as a Bigfoot sighting in those halcyon days of 2019—they got to talking.

It was a coincidence, certainly, but more than an accident. Synchronicity, Vik had called it. Random fucking luck that felt like the universe throwing them together, if they were willing to let it.

Eliza had received a double lung transplant only a year earlier. Vik was in the process of being listed for a new heart. They'd traded stories about hospitals, transplant, their entire medical histories, sharing intimate details as casually as a post-lecture question-and-answer. They bonded over the absolute improbability of the situation, the specifics of their lives: the cold entropy of disease, the eternal fight of being sick in America, of being walking scions of science and progress in an increasingly backwards and evangelical world. About anxieties and anger, lives stalled, dreams derailed, and the unquenchable hope for something better.

And then COVID happened and their worst fears were realized with screaming ferocity. Their hope snuffed out and scattered underfoot. Overnight, the world became a literal hell for the disabled and immuno-compromised, for people like them. The very air was poison, every person they passed a potential death sentence. And somehow it got worse from there. Anti-maskers, anti-vaxxers, the director of the goddamn CDC writing them off as acceptable collateral damage, smiling as she shrugged. Until, eventually, the world moved on, forgot, about the danger, about the virus—about Vik and Eliza entirely.

Until even doctors—their doctors, Eliza's doctors, the

same ones who'd coached her through transplant, who'd told her to treat the world as if it had been burning lava— couldn't be trusted to look out for her. Couldn't wear a mask, couldn't let her use telehealth, couldn't find ways to keep her out of waiting rooms lousy with contagion.

Until even friends and family abandoned her. Until her insistence that the pandemic was still happening, that everyone should continue to "take precautions" and "try not to kill her" drove them all to give up on her, to label her demanding or demented.

Until Vik and Eliza became each other's only support system.

Which made it all the stranger that Vik had retreated here. Had vanished to some island, with some guy, without telling Eliza *anything*. Vik was flighty some- times, sure, but not like this. Calls and texts never went *entirely* unanswered. The Snapchat message she'd received this morning, a straightforward order, was the first communication she'd had from her in months.

"What the fuck is going on, Vik?" Eliza asked.

"I don't know *what* you're talking about," Viktoriya answered, obviously lying. She began busying herself with the inspection of a nearby pillow. "I'm afraid you'll have to be more specific."

"*More specific?* Fine, okay, how about the goddamn gastrointestinal tract that just attacked me."

"A whole—"

"No, just a large intestine, appendix to rectum."

"Well, that's good."

"I don't think you and I use the same definition of that word."

"I am sorry that happened to you, Eliza. I didn't think—" Viktoriya paused, the manic fury of her old self briefly flashing to life. "Did you see anything else?"

"Else? What do you mean?"

"Any other organs?"

"There's more than one?!"

"Yes."

"What? How? Why? How many?"

"Well, you see—actually, for the sake of brevity, let us call it a heretofore unknown kind of galvanic radioactivity from a falling meteor. Like a defibrillator crashing to earth and charging the island. Interacting unexpectedly with the salt in the water and the soil. There's bodies all over."

"Why are there bodies all over, Vik?"

"Because Ingolstadt was—and I suppose is, technically, still—a pirate burial ground. Boot Hill for buccaneers, you could call it. The first Germans to land here built their settlement right over the top, and also named the island, obviously. I don't know whether they knew or not, whether it was intentional, but by the time the first resort was built in 1767—rudimentary, of course, mostly a sleepaway camp for the wealthy to escape all the summer diseases inland—I don't know if you know that, but that's how a lot of resorts in America and elsewhere began, as literal retreats for the rich from the very problems the rich were refusing to do anything about—but I don't think anyone suspected or noticed, not with all of them fleeing smallpox and yellow fever anyway."

"The intestine that attacked me wasn't old."

"Well, as I said, it was rejuvenated from the—"

"It was also holding a crowbar."

"Really? So they've moved on to using tools. Fascinating."

"Seriously, Vik, do you need a dictionary or—"

"They weren't using tools before." Viktoriya turned

to Clement, sitting on the arm of the sofa and sipping his coffee. "Were you aware of this? Have you seen evidence of this?"

"Only briefly," he replied, "while I was bringing Eliza inside."

"And it was *holding* a crowbar?"

"Wrapped itself around it like a tentacle."

"That would likely be the octopus DNA, yes."

"*What*," Eliza said.

"An octopus that washed up on the shore, probably, I mean," Viktoriya said. "And all the other octopi that are likely buried out there, the parts that the old Germans and earliest colonizers and all the tourists since didn't eat, that they excreted, and so on."

"I'm pretty sure none of that's true."

"Horseshoes and hand grenades, darling," she said with a dismissive wave of her hand, before turning back to Clement. "And have you documented this advancement?"

"Already in the ledger, yes," he replied.

There was something that Viktoriya wasn't telling Eliza—probably a lot of somethings, given the absolute batshittery of the situation—but now, she considered, wasn't the time for further inquiry. A single reanimated intestine was one thing, Eliza could deal with that—hell, half her time in grad school was spent finding new ways to make dead things twitch—but *multiple* organs, enough that Vik and Clement were keeping track of them? Multiple organs that seemed to be *gaining* intelligence? That were at least as smart as crows right now?

Whether it really was a *Night of the Living Dead* situation like Vik had said or something else—*What else could it be, though? An accident? An experiment? Why were they keeping notes?*—Eliza had no intention of sticking around and finding out.

"Look," she said, placing the vacuum-sealed bags of Egon's World onto the coffee table, "it's been a pleasure meeting you and Gentleman Jeeves here, but I gotta get going. Aside from nearly being maimed by a colon, there's a storm a'comin' and I'd rather not be caught in the open water when it does. Or outside. Or anywhere other than my apartment, honestly."

"You could stay here," Viktoriya offered.

Clement cleared his throat.

"Oh, hush," she replied, patting his leg. "What's the point of having this house if we're not going to host guests? At least one of the rooms is still made up, isn't it?"

"I appreciate the offer, Vik, but I gotta get home and do my meds."

"Nonsense, Eliza. You and I are taking the same prescriptions, or at least the important ones, and I always keep extra on hand. A month ahead on all my refills at all times. It's the only way to have true peace of mind! And if I'm wrong—which I'm not—missing *one* dose won't kill you."

"Well, I've also got ... plans tonight?" Eliza stood. "A date? A flight I need to catch? I don't know, some kind of unassailable commitment that gets me away from this island of zombie pirate innards." She smiled. "I'm sure you understand. Have fun expounding each other!"

Clement, leaning forward, inched the tray across the coffee table, closer to Eliza.

"At least take some cookies for your big night alone with your laptop and your empty apartment and whatever battery-operated boyfriend you're feeling up to," he said, nudging the tray again. "Oatmeal raisin. They're fresh-baked."

INFERNAL ORGANS

Eliza narrowed her eyes at him.

Then: "Yeah, all right."

The rain was already starting to fall, thin but constant, a ragged veil of curling mist. Eliza made her way back down the old palmetto path—quickly and cautiously this time, eyes constantly scanning, keys threaded through her fingers—toward her boat, the shitty little fishing dinghy she'd borrowed from a dock along the shore.

Ingolstadt was a barrier island, the farthest east in South Carolina, separated from the rest of Charleston's beaches and resort islands by a narrow inlet. Eliza could see the condos and vacation homes, the massive hotel of Wild Dunes, on the far shore. Lined up, lit up. Sparkling like jewels in the night. Pretty, even from here.

There was, Eliza was only now realizing, a good chance the boat she took had been a decoration.

"Reason number two not to do this while stoned, dum-dum," she mumbled, munching on one of Clement's cookies. "Let's just hope it survives the ten minutes it takes to—"

She stopped, frozen, maybe ten feet from the muddy shoreline.

The boat wasn't there.

At least, not as anything identifiable as a boat.

The entire thing was in pieces, portions, particles. Taken apart, dismantled, slat by slat and screw by screw, reduced to a few neat and knolled piles of lumber and hardware.

And it had been done by crabs.

By dozens of tiny, white crabs.

This was, dear reader, obviously *not* what had taken apart the boat. You've seen the cover, you can read the headers. You know what this book is. But Eliza Duran did not have access to that information, and, as a result, her brain was having a very hard time processing what she was seeing, and not just because of the pot.

—no, nope. Are you fucking—

Eyeballs. The crabs were *eyeballs*. Dozens of them, dozens of eyeballs—white and globular, a variety of sizes, a rainbow of irises catching the dim cloudlight, the last efforts of the straining sun—dozens of eyeballs inchworming across the silty sand with their optic nerves, thick and wending, wriggling, crosshatching the dark beach. Wielding screwdrivers and rusted knives, prying loose boards and twisting out attachments. Eyeballs—*so many fucking eyeballs*—moving as one methodical, co-ordinated unit, like ants packing up a picnic.

Ironically, they didn't seem to see her.

Eliza, dropping her cookie, turned and started running anyway.

"Hey, Vik!" she shouted. "Vik! Clement! Open the door!"

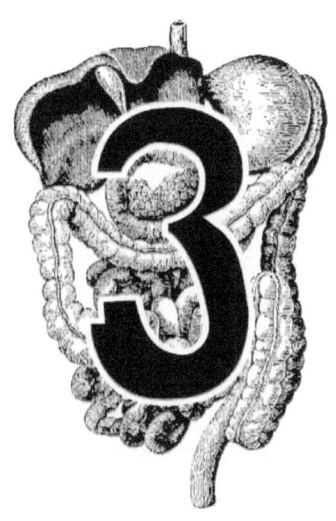

"... AND THIS IS YOUR ROOM."

Eliza was holding an enormous mug of coffee with both hands, an equally enormous blanket draped over her shoulders and arms and trailing behind her, exchanged for her hoodie and bag. She and Clement were on the third or maybe the fourth floor; honestly, she wasn't paying attention. Despite all the rare and expensive tchotchkes and architectural idiosyncrasies Clement kept pointing out, Eliza wasn't quite up for marveling at the house anymore, for what she felt were fairly obvious reasons.

One freak organ attack, *fine*. Bodies couldn't be trusted and life was fucking weird. Eliza knew that better than almost anyone. This wasn't even the first time an intestine had tried to kill her, technically. But a hockey team's worth of eyeballs dismantling a boat, working together, in unison?

And yet Vik and Clement had barely reacted. Sure, a

few eyebrows were cocked and mental notes had been made that the organs had moved from simple tool usage to advanced, but mostly they'd busied themselves with welcoming her back to the manor like she was a family member visiting from out of town. Like she hadn't been forced into the house by uncanny anatomy twice now.

"... sconces from Vienna," Clement was saying, "imported during ..."

The only part of the tour that had left any kind of impression on Eliza was that most of the rooms on the lower floors—the ones not in immediate use anyway—had been meticulously deconstructed. Entire walls were missing, revealing janky skeleton frames of not nearly enough two-by-fours, of wiring stripped and snipped into sprouts. Pieces of furniture sat in piles on the floor; heavy drapes had been shredded into thin strips.

The barricade had to come from somewhere, she supposed.

Buoyed by that thought, by the modicum of safety the fence brought, by being inside and off the ground floor, Eliza sat down on the bounteous four-poster bed and let herself untense. Waited for her hands to stop shaking, for the adrenaline to leave. Looking out the room's oriel window, she could see nearly the whole of the other side of the island, the august anterior, the showy lawn, as ostentatious as a golf course, and about the same size, too. Mapped out, manicured to the millimeter, for tourists and photographers.

Strings of fairy lights and clusters of paper lanterns, threaded from patio to post across the island, danced in the wind, the growing dark. Thick and slumping vines of jessamine crawled along artfully askew fences, lining the beach. Pink plumes of sweetgrass, fading with the early winter, tufted atop small hillocks. And, in the center, lined up precisely, interlocking like puzzle pieces, were the spreading, weeping branches of a dozen live oaks—trees as old as the world and twice as knotted—arched across the cobblestone path to the ferry dock.

Eliza wondered how much reanimated offal was hiding in the shadows. She wondered how much more advanced the organs would become in the next hour, the next twelve.

She wondered how the fuck she was gonna get off this island.

Maybe she could call the ferry—the sightseeing ferry that meandered to Dewees Island and the Isle of Palms, to the sound beyond, the suburban shores of Mount Pleasant eventually—what was the company's name? Or maybe she could find a charter boat, schedule a pick-up. Reception on the island was absolute shit, but Vik had to have wi-fi, right? Or at least a phonebook and a landline. How long would that take? Too long, probably. It was late and getting later; any potential rescuers likely wouldn't head out until morning. Maybe she could swim? The storm and the cold would make sure any attempt sucked six kinds of ass, but the inlet wasn't *that* wide.

That's when a small lighthouse, perched on a high, rocky outcropping to the north, switched on. In the flash of rotating light, Eliza saw a boathouse beside and beneath the tower, nestled into a crevice of the dark rock.

Or, at least, she *thought* she did. The inconstant light, the rain—or was it snow now?—made it difficult to see, to focus. But there had to be a boat, right? For emergencies? No rich fuck was going to patiently sit here with so much as a papercut, waiting for the ferry.

Eliza turned toward Clement, still standing in the

hallway, and saw for the first time the room opposite hers. Another bedroom, nearly identical, save for the color. An older man, probably in his sixties, stocky and abraded by age, was sitting in an armchair, head back and snoring.

"Has he been there this whole time?"

"He has. That's Ernest," Clement explained. "Groundskeeper, caretaker, and handyman for the resort. I'd introduce you, but he's had a long couple of days and it's generally ill-advised to wake him."

"I'll bet. Is he all right, though? He's *really* out."

"Oh, certainly. This is what he does—his process, if you will. I daresay he only *exists* in between jobs. He's a wonderful worker, clever, industrious, and then he is simply done, scarcely conscious save to snack or shit, if you'll pardon the crass alliteration, for days on end. There's frankly nothing in the middle. He's been at the manor since he was sixteen, but I couldn't tell you a single thing about him."

"Since he was sixteen? How long have you—"

The lights went out then, the entire estate blinked into darkness. Silence shuddered into being as the thrum of appliances and electricity ceased suddenly, the resulting absence falling like a thunderclap.

"Oh, what the fuck now?" Eliza mumbled.

"The others," Clement replied, "will likely be asking the same question."

"Others?"

"The rest of our guests."

"Of course," she said.

Because that's what this strange, shit-ass night needed. People. Huddled masses of rich, entitled fucks taking a vacation whenever the fuck they wanted, scouting the island to see if they wanted to have the entire family out here for Christmas or some shit, or maybe holding a business retreat the way some offices had pizza parties. If there was any upside—and she was *extremely* hesitant to agree that there was—at least all those Richie Riches had probably been vaccinated with the most up-to-date, gold-plated, made-from-the-tears-of-the-poor serum out there.

Clement shifted an eyebrow, an almost microscopic movement, but one that Eliza nonetheless knew meant there would be no politely declining the invitation.

"Are there still cookies?" she asked.

"In the oven as we speak."

Sighing, Eliza pulled a folded N95 out of her back pocket.

Ingolstadt Island's smattering of off-season visitors were gathered at Grimke Manor within the hour, mingling with subdued merriment in the gold-and-burgundy parlor. The heating and electric had, in the mansion, at least, restarted shortly after going out. The manor was the biggest house on the island by a wide margin, and had several generators; the welcome binders in the rental cottages made a point of directing guests here in an emergency. The temperament of the room was somewhere between annoyance and amusement: the island's electricity was old and wonky, that was part of the draw, and damaging storms weren't exactly a foreign occurrence along the South Carolina coast. No one could be *too* upset.

So long as the situation was resolved quickly anyway.

The most pronounced of the gathered was, for all the wrong reasons, one Billiam Ackerman, followed in short order by his fellow douchebuddies Beckett, Blake, Bradley, Brooks, and Bryce. Whether they were tech-bros or Wall Street turds, Eliza couldn't tell. But they were loud and laughing, taking up as much space as possible, both physically and figuratively. The six of them— standing with legs spread and chests out, or leaning too-casually on every random fixture they could—were clumped together by the fireplace, and still overpowering the not-inconsequential room. In attitude and app-earance, they were practically identical, save for the occasional change of ethnicity or skin tone: short hair slicked to the side; slim-fit jeans and too-tight Oxfords, a fleece vest with the collar turned up, so you knew they were off-the-clock. Any actual differences between them were purely academic, took effort to discern, like a dentist's office magazine puzzle. She couldn't tell you which one had made the snide remark about her mask, but it didn't really matter; they'd all snickered the same.

Sitting quietly on the sofa were Carol and Alf McClanahan, a married couple, white as mayonnaise with hair the exact same shade of slate gray. Alf was almost painfully straightlaced, gruff, stoic, and built like a refrig-erator; "former military" seemed to be his entire person-ality. Carol, meanwhile, a paper butterfly of a woman, sitting patiently with her hands in her lap, looked like she was auditioning for a revival of *The Donna Reed Show*.

And then there was Justina Moore, a *very* Southern ASMRtist—a YouTuber who whispered strangers to sleep—trying to engage Eliza in conversation, on at least three different topics at once, only without ever pausing long enough to let Eliza speak. Not that Eliza minded all that much: Justina was gorgeous and charming, with skin like porcelain, hair like midnight, curled like the '40s, and a lilting drawl she could listen to all day. She was wearing a long skirt and a loose, ruffled top. Had pale blue acrylic nails, tastefully decorated with snowmen. Nervous energy radiated off of her, adorable instead of awkward, though, a Disney princess who'd had too much coffee. Everything about Justina screamed "trying too hard," but in a way that made you want to try harder, too.

"I can't tell if you're real or an offensive stereotype," Eliza said, goggling at the young woman standing before her.

"You're so funny!" Justina replied, followed by a laugh like a hog in shit, a series of snorts so enormous her entire voluptuous body contorted and contracted like an accordion to get them all out.

Eliza was willing to bet *that* didn't go into the sleepy-time videos.

There was movement over Justina's shoulder; Eliza saw another man crossing the foyer hurriedly, shaking off snow from his jacket as he moved. Clement, having presumably lifted open the barricade hatch for him and locked the door after, followed him into Eliza's line of sight.

The man was middle-aged, white, in his fifties maybe, well-dressed and too-casual simultaneously, in a two-hundred-dollar hoodie kind of way. An enormous fedora sat high on his head; it should've looked ridiculous, but somehow didn't. He was familiar, too. Eliza knew she had a habit of filtering things through pop culture—to paraphrase *Community's* Jeff Winger, *television* never abandoned you—but this guy *really* looked like he could have been *Justified's* Walton Goggins.

He immediately went to the other parlor, on the far side of the foyer, the overly blue one with the bar. He was moving in a way that suggested this drink was more therapeutic than social, moving the way Eliza had when she'd arrived the second time, too many emotions barely contained.

He saw something out there.

He was, however, the only one who had.

Despite the fact that they'd all climbed through a fucking fence, a homemade rampart covered in jagged metal and broken glass, the gathered seemed only to regard this assemblage as an impromptu "power's out!" party. None of them had reported feeling any particularly creepy vibes, nor seeing things moving in the shadows. No eyeballs, no large intestines with crowbars, or, what, spleens with brass knuckles or something. There was no fear, no paranoia, no frantic glances. If Eliza were to ask them, any of them, the answer would undoubtedly be the same: there was absolutely *nothing* outside. Save, perhaps, for the run-of-the-mill unsettling of the soul that accompanied trudging through the dark and the snow and the wind.

But Walton Goggins saw something.

Eliza began the process of politely extricating herself from Justina's presence—no need to set that bridge on fire, especially when she hadn't stiffened the beams and snapped the suspensions herself yet—with the intent of joining Walton at the bar, only to be interrupted by the evening's hosts. Viktoriya and Clement were standing side-by-side beneath the foyer arch, blocking Eliza's way. There was something about their manner, their body language; Eliza knew Vik well enough to know something was amiss.

Y'know, besides the obvious.

After a moment, and the readjustment of her demeanor, Viktoriya stepped into the parlor, raising a fancy glass of what appeared to be absinthe, and tapped it with an equally fancy spoon.

"Hello, my friends!" she called out, as if everything was right as rain. "Thank you all so much for coming out, though I do wish this meeting was under better circumstances. As I am sure you're no doubt aware, the inclement weather seems to have caused a small hiccup with the island's electrical substation. But, please, don't worry: Grimke Manor is equipped with backup generators and backups to the backups, for just such an issue! And our stalwart superintendent Ernest is on the case as we speak, and will have the power in your cottages up and humming in two shakes! In the meantime, please do make yourselves comfortable here."

"You're really going to send him out there?" Eliza asked, unquietly, in front of everyone—and much to the immediately noticeable annoyance of Viktoriya and Clement. "Ernie?"

"Why *wouldn't* send him out there?' Viktoriya asked.

"He has snow boots," Clement added.

"Because of the—" Eliza stopped abruptly. All eyes were on her, even Walton Goggins' from the foyer. She turned around to confirm the feeling, to face the rest of the guests, and immediately regretted the action.

It had been so long since she'd been in a group setting—so long since she'd been around more than one or two people, people that she knew well—had been so long since she'd had to engage in anything more than idle chitchat as she delivered various drugs—that she'd forgotten how to act. Forgotten that blurting out every random thought to her cat wasn't how actual people had actual conversations. She was suddenly extremely self-conscious, and she hadn't even gotten to the part where she was trying to tell a room full of rich folks there were zombie organs outside trying to murder everyone.

"Because of the wild animals," Viktoriya said, putting a hand on Eliza's shoulder as she stepped beside her. "Yes, that's it, wild animals. Let's say, I don't know, squirrels. A whole nest of squirrels seem to have stowed away on the ferry and migrated here. They are all very rabid, however, so, please, keep your distance. One of them already gave Eliza quite the scare."

"I love squirrels!" Justina squeed, clapping her hands together.

"You *cannot* be a real person," Eliza said.

"In any event," said Clement, stepping along Eliza's other side, "please enjoy the coffee and cookies and make yourself at home. We should have you all back to your cottages shortly." He looked at Eliza. "As long as there are no more *squirrel* attacks, that is."

Eliza bristled.

"We need to get out of here," she said, practically growling. "If we can call a charter—" She turned to the guests again, toward Carol and Alf specifically. "—or if one of you, I guess, brought your own boat—that's a thing people who vacation at private resorts have, right?—if one of you—"

Billiam had sidled up behind her, was pressing himself close.

"I'll take you wherever you're trying to go, ba—"

Eliza's fist, with extreme prejudice, found his testicles. He doubled over and staggered sideways, before falling to his knees and dry-heaving into the fireplace. His douchebuddies crowded around him, cooing platitudes and epithets and staring at Eliza as if she'd dropkicked a baby. Justina, meanwhile, fought back a snicker.

"I think I saw a boathouse," Eliza continued, calmer,

"by the lighthouse. If we can get to it without the—the *squirrels*—finding us, we can get out of here. Maybe, if we all go as a group—"

A hand clamped over Eliza's mouth. It was Viktoriya.

"Oh, the imagination on this one!" she said. "Please forgive her; she was a theater major. Always on, always so *dramatic*, you know how it is." Then, to Eliza, even as she was already dragging the delivery woman into the next room: "A word, yes? I think we have some things to discuss."

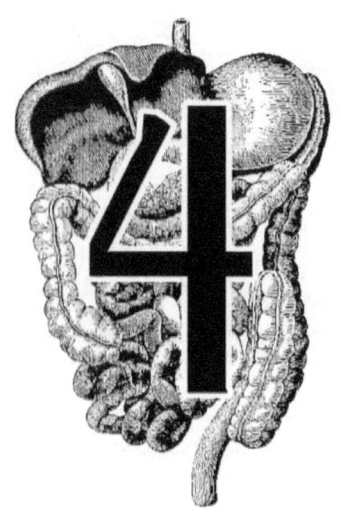

"WHAT THE FUCK IS GOING ON WITH YOU?" Eliza practically shouted. They were in the kitchen—like, a Gordon Ramsey-style kitchen, bigger and more well-appointed than her apartment. "Why aren't you telling them the truth?"

"To what end?" Viktoriya replied, a hand gesticulating the question. She was leaning, slouching, against a steel counter so clean it was basically a mirror. "So we have ten more people losing their minds and trying to flee? I mean, escape—*leave*." She smiled. "Eliza," she purred, "think this through. You tried to leave once, and it didn't work. This, here, Grimke Manor, it's the safest place on this island."

"We've gone out of our way to ensure that," Clement added.

"Yeah, about that," Eliza said. "What is this, really? What's going on here?"

The more she thought about it, the less and less likely the defibrillator-meteor theory seemed—and it had seemed like a big ol' pile of horseshit to start with. What could bring organs to life like that, with consciousness, or at least purpose? There was too much weird shit happening, and, after the eyeballs, after Walton Goggins got spooked, too, it was feeling less and less accidental.

"The truth, Viktoriya," she said.

"The organs ..." Viktoriya started, staring at the floor.

"Vik, are you sure?" Clement said.

"Oh, she deserves to know. Eliza's as much a part of this as you or I. I mean, not *as much*, no, obviously, but, philosophically, spiritually—we were going to have to tell her sooner or later."

"What are you talking about?" Eliza demanded.

"Please know that I did this for you, Elizabeth," Viktoriya said, stepping forward and taking Eliza's hands in her own. "You know that, in the past, I have dabbled in experimentation. Usually, to no end, to no *meaningful* success, but, well, this time was different. This time, with Clement's help, I finally—

"I have had *issues* with my health," she continued, "ever since my heart transplant. You know this. I've not be quiet about it, I know. Rejection, infection, the thickening of my coronary arteries, having to keep my distance from other people, all of their weird diseases and bacteria, having to wear a mask—"

"You're not wearing a mask," Eliza said.

"—to constantly protect myself from them. An allergy to *humanity* in all but name. Forced seclusion. For my own good, my own safety. It was harder for me than for others—than for you, for example."

This, at least, was true. Eliza had certainly had her own share of transplant troubles—her own infections, scarring on her lungs, a C. diff scare that nearly killed her, countless other intrapersonal lessons hard-learned—but she was younger and able to bounce back more quickly. And, the loss of her job notwithstanding—her inability to be in an office where everyone refused to cover their mouths when they sneezed, that kept confiscating her air filters because of some nebulously-enforced dictate of professional homogeny—being immunocompromised was, really, a gift to her introverted self. An excuse to be the hermit she'd always aspired to be.

Viktoriya took a deep breath. "I was trying to create a better organ, Eliza. A better heart. One that wouldn't fight back, so to speak. A topical unguent that—I'd wanted to build brand-new organs from scratch, that's what everyone else is doing, trying for—artificial what-have-yous—but that takes so long, and there are so many intricacies that need to be contended with, so many tiny things that can and will go wrong. So, the salve, instead, a modulating bridge between old and new.

"The problem with transplant, beyond the violence of the surgery, is, as I'm certain you already know, that you are inherently placing a square peg in a round hole. Placing innards from Person A into the outtards of Person B. But you can't have someone else's organs—foreign objects for all intents and purposes—inside another body; the immune system will view them as antagonists and attack accordingly. Hence all the drugs we're on, to lower the ferocity of that attack—" She smiled grimly. "—and leave us susceptible to every other goddamn thing out there.

"But the salve, Eliza, the salve binds to the donor organ and modifies the proteins along the organ's surface, identifying residual markers in the pleural cavity and pericardium, matching itself to them before replicating. Before *building*, creating a serous membrane, a porous shell, twinned with the countless others already in the recipient's body. Additional daily supplementation, delivered via a timed-release capsule—a pill, Eliza, *one pill*—would instigate the lengthier process of rewriting the donor organ itself. But the salve—*the salve!*—think of it as genetic camouflage, hiding the new heart within the detritus of the old one, buying time when transplantees are at their most vulnerable, and avoiding the issues of rejection and immunosuppression altogether.

"I was trying to make the transplant experience easier for the recipients, better, for you and for me. For all of us, and everyone after. Trying to find a way to avoid the years of struggle, the hospital visits, the opportunistic infections that seem to lurk around every corner, the trading of a coronary disease for one involving the immune system. I was trying to create the life we were promised, the one we suffered and died and came back for—I was trying to make that life one we could actually *live*. And—

"—and I did, Eliza. *We* did, Clement and I. The salve *worked*. We created, in essence, a universal organ. No more rejection. No more infection. And, more than that, we shortened the wait time. Made finding a match easier, quicker. Size is, still, certainly an issue—one remains unable to transplant the lungs of a basketball player into the body of a little girl—but so much of the other bloodwork, the infinitesimal marrying of this and that, is no longer needed. You are, no doubt, aware of the abysmal *statistics*—" She spat the word. "—regarding deaths while waiting for a compatible organ, while on the transplant list. But no more. We fixed the whole damn thing, Eliza. Upended everything the world knows about organ transplant, but this time—this time!—with the patients' needs first."

"That—that's amazing," Eliza said. She knew she should probably have more to say than that, but, truthfully, she was struggling with the enormity of the confession. If this was real, if Vik and Clement had really done it, then it was monumental. Life-altering. Nothing would be the same.

But was it true? She wanted it to be, certainly, but where was the evidence? Why, instead of smiling transplantees, instead of hospital administrators breaking down the door with bags full of money, were there senti- ent, tool-wielding organs prowling around the island?

"Why are they attacking?" Eliza asked. "The organs. Why are they *alive*?"

"Well, that ..." Vik scrunched up her face. "That's the unfortunate part."

"Our trial tests were a bit *too* successful," Clement said. "Without a pleural cavity to draw guidance from, without a body to contain them, the unguent adapted to quite literally everything else, to the very world itself, to fire, water, earth, and air. Allowing the organs to, well, breathe, for lack of a better term. To function and survive independently."

"But that's why you're here," Viktoriya said, "that's why everyone's here. We need to finish our experiment, Eliza. But more work is more time is ... not to be gauche, but more money." Viktoriya stepped closer to Clement, wrapping her arm around his waist. "Clement here is a scientist, too, world-renowned in certain circles. This is his island; his lab is downstairs. Cutting-edge and fully- loaded, like a baked potato from the future. But to afford that, well, grants only go so far. So he supplements his research with rich tourists, with angel investors and

Silicon Valley-types, the kinds who soil themselves upon hearing the word 'disruption.' Who spend first and think later. Everyone out there is *obscenely* wealthy."

"Honestly," Clement added, "you mention the words 'artificial intelligence' and they've already got their digital pocketbooks at the ready. Never mind that the intelligence in question is meat-based, accidental, and the very thing you're trying to solve."

"And me?" Eliza asked. "Why am I here?"

"Well, the cannabis, darling," Viktoriya answered. "How am I to quiet my anxieties? My fears? How am I to tap into the collective unconscious, to expand my mind far enough to find a solution, if I'm *sober*? You, Eliza, are the most important part."

"After the scientific equipment and the money, that is," Clement said.

"Right, obviously. But, still: top three!"

Eliza took a moment to reflect on all she'd been told. She had her doubts—oodles of them, frankly—but she'd also seen the proof in the squirming, violent flesh. The science wasn't precisely *sound*, but it was plausible enough. Nanotech had, at least in prototypes, the ability to engineer human tissue, and she was herself on a trio of drugs that worked as protein modulators, rewriting the faulty genes at the core of her cystic fibrosis. And *something* had brought those organs to life, unleashed them, so why not this?

"Okay," she said after a moment, "so, on board, but two questions first."

"Shoot," Viktoriya said.

"One, how many organs are there? How many trials did you run?"

"Well," she replied, counting on her fingers, "we started with the eyes, there were, roughly, thirty-six of them, that was the first trial. The large intestine was next, there were three of them. And then the heart, obviously, I think there were six when all was said and done. You'll have to trust that there was a method to our madness, dear, one driven more by supply than demand than we would have preferred, but that is the nature of guerrilla experimentation, no?"

"Sure. But that's it, right? You didn't run any more tests?"

"Not a one."

"Not after we figured out what was happening," Clement added.

"Not after the eyeballs started *walking*," Viktoriya elaborated. "Working together. Planning a daring escape liked they'd been harvested from Steve McQueen himself."

"Please don't remind me," Eliza said. "I am extremely unlikely to *ever* forget that. Eyeballs are gross and surreal enough even when they're not ambulatory. And ... building tiny boats? Is that what we think they were doing when they took apart mine?"

"Based on the available evidence, and the fact that they're all pirate eyes—buccaneer Boot Hill and the peculiarities of the bog-like soil here have been absolutely instrumental to our efforts—that much from earlier *was* accurate—but, again, as they're pirate eyes with some semblance of seafaring cellular memory in there somewhere, a careful *yes*. Why the hell not, right?"

"Okay. Sketchy, but, yeah. Which brings us to B: why can't *we* leave?"

"Ah, well, that's the awkward part," Clement explained. "The donors out there—the financial donors—they haven't technically *agreed* just yet. I have meetings with all of them scheduled over the next few days, an opportunity for the hard sell and the formal requests, dot the i's and cross the t's—*after* we wine them and dine them for a bit, naturally."

"So you can see," Viktoriya added, "how scaring them away *before* they've heard the pitch would not be in anyone's best interests."

There were, in fact, countless ways that fleeing an island crawling with several dozen sentient organs would indeed be in *everyone's* best interests, but trying to untangle scientific progress from capitalism seemed beyond the ken of both Eliza and a single conversation. And, more to the point, who actually cared if some independently wealthy shitlord got brained by a colon? Fuck the rich.

"Okay, fine," Eliza agreed. "But why can't *I* leave?"

"Because of the snow and your lack of transportation?" Clement replied, genuine confusion on his face. "I know you're still relatively new to South Carolina, but I was under the impression New Jersey did also have beaches and storms. The ferry won't be in operation until the weather clears. I would imagine most charters are the same."

"What about the boathouse?"

"What boathouse?"

"By the lighthouse?"

"I am not aware of any such thing," he replied, "but then I do scarcely leave the island these days, ever since the dawn of the internet. I suppose there could be a boat of some kind, but you would have to ask Ernest, and I'm afraid he's across the island trying to get the power back on."

"Honestly," Viktoriya said, "you're acting like spending a weekend in an opulent mansion is a punishment."

"Hyperintelligent organs and rich assholes aren't my idea of fun."

"Again, Eliza," Clement said, "Grimke Manor is fortified. As long as you stay inside, you will be absolutely fine. Ernie and I have made certain of that. I have no inclination to risk my own life and limb either."

"Please, dear," Viktoriya said, "find some way to enjoy yourself."

Eliza ran her tongue over her back teeth.

Enjoy herself, huh?

"So, Justina ... she's here alone?"

If life was so hellbent on handing Eliza lemons, the least she could do was squeeze 'em, and maybe some watermelons, too, have herself a little agua fresca. That's not a great metaphor—agua fresca's actually made with limes, not lemons, especially with watermelon—but you get my drift.

"No," Clement said, "no sleeping with anyone. Viktoriya has told me of your sullied romantic past. Your proclivity to 'fuck and run' is, I think, the vernacular?"

"I would *never*."

"Well, good, because I've seen the way you were looking at Justina."

"She's like a sexist comic-book drawing come to life. Or an Instagram fitness person, where the tits and ass are always on the same side somehow, following you around the room like a haunted painting."

"Keep it in your pants, Eliza," Viktoriya scolded.

"And maybe keep it to *one* metaphor going forward," Clement added.

"Okay, yes," Eliza said, "but—and hear me out—what if I sleep with her now, and keep sleeping with her until *after* she signs whatever you need her to sign. Call it sweetening the honeypot. Win-win-win."

"Hm." Clement furrowed his brow. "That's not a *terrible* idea. Justina is the most skittish of the investors, looking to expand her online empire, to do more with her money, but, as yet, in no particularly focused way. You're certain you'd be able to keep her interested and happy that whole time?"

"Absofuckinlutely," Eliza said, grinning. "There's no way a woman that Southern has ever actually gotten off before. The difficult part's gonna be getting rid of her after."

"Well, in that case—"

A blood-curdling shriek erupted from the other room.

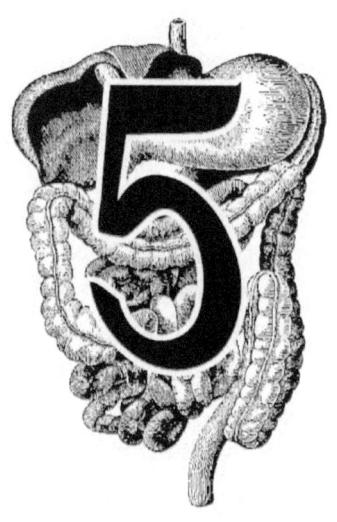

BILLIAM ACKERMAN WAS LYING DEAD ON THE FLOOR, his throat roughly slit, jagged skin fluttering over burbling blood like an unhemmed curtain in a slight breeze. With each spurt, the blood pooled thicker around the dead man's head, stretching and seeping into the nearly-as-red throw rug.

Justina was kneeling over him, holding her blood-soaked hands to her face, eyes white and wide with horror. The girl and the body were on the far side of the parlor, near the entrance to the next room, the half-ruined piano room, away from Eliza, Vik, Clement, and everyone else. The Christmas tree towered over them, glowing like an electrocuted clown.

"You killed him!" Blake shouted, pointing an accusatory finger. He and his fellow douchebuddies were still huddled near the fireplace, clutching closer in fury and confoundment. "You killed him! You bitch!"

"I didn't," Justina cried. "I swear! I swear it wasn't me!"

"Then who was it, huh? Who killed Billiam?"

"I don't—well, I don't know. But it wasn't me!"

"Liar!" Blake shouted. "You can't even come up with a good excuse!"

"I'm sorry," Eliza interrupted, holding out her hands and stepping between the warring factions, "you really think this sweet dummy of a YouTuber murdered your boy? In cold blood? In front of everyone?"

"We can't hear you over your mask," Bryce said.

Eliza ignored him. "You think this walking ray of sugar-coated sunshine, this adorable, living kawaii drawing, this hyper-realistic Betty Boop of an individual—"

"Thank you?" Justina snuffled.

"—did literally anything that would make someone unhappy?"

"Well, *someone* killed him," Beckett replied. "He didn't cut his own throat. And Scarlett O'Hara over there was standing next to him, talking to him. And, historically, that upsets females like you for some reason. Talking to him. You don't like that—

"So many females have threatened to kill him," said Bryce.

"So many," Bradley added.

"— so, habeas corpus, it was her!"

Justina ran over to Eliza, burying her sobbing face in Eliza's shoulder.

"Did you at least wipe off the blood?" Eliza asked.

"No," Justina replied, sniffling and not looking up.

Eliza sighed. "All right, well, what happened then?"

"I don't know!" Justina removed herself from Eliza's arms, a stream of snot connecting them briefly before breaking. She turned toward the body. "He was talking to me, kind of gross and aggressive, and so I was trying to get out of the conversation, but he wouldn't let me, he kept following me around the room, but then I heard something, like—like a cat walking across a piano or something—and I turned, toward the piano and the noise, but I didn't see anything, and then I turned back, and he was—he was bleeding and gasping and choking and—and dying!" She threw herself into Eliza again. "*And now he's dead!*"

Eliza, ignoring the voluminous tears and nasal secretions once again soaking into her long-sleeved t-shirt, held Justina close and warm and began rubbing her back.

"There," she said to the douchebuddies. "She didn't do it."

"Oh, and we're supposed to trust *you*?" Brooks replied. "The other one?"

"What am I, chopped liver?" asked Carol, sitting six inches from Eliza.

"You already punched him in the dick once!" Bryce added, ignoring Carol because she was a woman over forty. Seriously, reader, he didn't see her, didn't hear her. *Literally* did not, could not. As far as he and the rest of the douchebuddies were concerned, Alf was sitting on the sofa and looking disinterested all by himself.

"She killed him!" Brooks said.

"And now we're going to kill her!" Beckett shouted.

"Wait, what?" Eliza said.

"Yeah," said Bryce, "yeah!" He was starting to hop in place, getting himself all worked up. "Who's going to stop us, huh? Some female?" He waved a hand toward Clement (and Viktoriya), standing beneath the foyer arch. "That beta male cuck wearing an apron and making us all brownies?"

"In fact," said Clement, "many of the world's foremost pastry chefs—"

"C'mon, get serious, dude."

"Let's get her!" one of the others shouted.

"Yeah!"

"Let's commit a murder!"

"And then pay some cops to cover it up!"

"Woo!"

The five nearly-identical businessholes started toward Eliza and Justina, laughing amongst themselves, circling out and closing in like a pack of hyenas. Eliza, backing up into the sofa, couldn't help but feel that the young men's obvious failings as human beings were suddenly a lot more threatening, and a lot harder to dismiss.

"This is our house now!" Bryce shouted, banging his fist against his chest. "Our house! We're—"

A brain appeared on Bryce's shoulder.

"Huh? What is that?" He turned his head, but, due to the thickness of his neck and the height of his collar, couldn't quite see. His douchebuddies were similarly of no help, only pointing and stuttering.

Eliza scrambled to come up with a joke about them not recognizing a brain—maybe something about the Scarecrow from *The Wizard of Oz*—but her attempted witticism was too slow, hampered by the unpleasant thought that, if she was in the mind to joke, then she must have been getting used to the sentient organs. And normalizing randomly-appearing body parts didn't feel like a particularly healthy thing to do.

The brain—a vaguely-shaped blob of slopping gray matter slouching on Bryce's shoulder like bird shit—pulled a rusted hacksaw into view. Various arteries, the paramedian and lateral bulbars, red as a devil, and nerves as fine as spiderwebs were wrapped around the wooden handle, lifting it from behind Bryce's back—

—and placing the jagged blade in front of his neck.

"Oh, God, is it a squirrel? One of those rabid squirrels?" He was spinning futilely, like a dog chasing his tail. "I swear to our Lord and Savior Elon Musk, if this thing bites me—" He turned to his friends. "—if you let this thing bite me—" He turned toward Clement (and Viktoriya). "—I will sue you and this entire island into *oblivion*."

"Will you now?" Clement said, a smirk kinking his lips.

"This is a weird time to be smug, bro," Brooks said.

"Is it?"

And then, slowly, each rusted tooth tearing skin with excruciating effort, the brain slit Bryce's throat, too. Blood flowed from his neck like a waterfall. Still thinking it was a squirrel, a scratch, he tried to catch the blood in his hands, tried to, with the panicked horror of dawning realization, put it back in, babbling as he bled out.

"Jesus," Eliza mumbled.

Everyone else, meanwhile, was screaming.

Panic overwhelmed the parlor, descending like a goddamn avalanche. The douchebuddies—staring in shock as Bryce fell to his knees between them, as he expired and toppled to the hardwood floor—as the hacksaw-wielding brain hopped onto Bryce's back and began looking around, scouting for its next victim—shouted expletive-laden epithets in unison, then scattered, spreading like buckshot. One of them fled directly into an end table, knocking a Tiffany lamp to the ground, before falling into and over the couch. Carol and Alf were already gone, having retreated to the foyer; they were currently clawing at one another, muttering *What do we do? What do we do?* over and over. Behind them, Walton Goggins was throwing his weight against the front door, struggling to keep it closed, boots skidding along the marble. On either side of him, windows were rattling, moments from giving way.

Clement and Viktoriya were nowhere to be found.

Justina, however, was very much there, screeching and half-crouched, wanting desperately to back away, to be literally anywhere else. She was grabbing at Eliza's hand, attempting to pull her along, too.

But Eliza—scientific inquiry and lower-class vengeance and, yes, a growing acceptance of murderous organs, plus a hospital-honed tolerance for blood and body horror, all getting the best of her—wanted to watch.

One of the panicking douchebuddies—let's say Bradley; Bradley was one of them, right?—had run back to the fireplace and grabbed the iron poker, was, currently, his back to the hearth, brandishing it like a longsword. And behind him? A trio of small intestines, all twenty-plus feet of them, pink and beige and wet, flopping around like empty hot dog casings as they dropped down from the flue.

Before Eliza could think to say anything—before she could even decide if she really wanted to, given the victim—the intestines shot out from the fireplace and wrapped themselves around Bradley's arms and legs and waist, constricting tightly. Flailing feebly, bending only at his wrists, at one slightly-less-constricted elbow, his hands pulled futilely on the elastic organs, the offal stretching and snapping against his fingers as if they were workout bands.

Then the intestines retreated back up the flue, pulling the young man up, up, up, like the Grinch stealing a Christmas tree, only with a lot more screaming and blood. Sickening cracks, the sound of bones snapping and shattering, echoed out of the fireplace. Bits of Bradley scraped against the chimney's interior, sloughing off and falling back down in clouds of shoot.

Eliza jolted suddenly sideways, carried off-balance by a tug on her arm. Rage warmed through her, automatic. A sensorial instinct against surprise, yet another idiosyncrasy honed by years in and out of hospitals, by nothing but bad news coming when you weren't ready. Any lingering whisps of revulsion and terror coalesced into fury; her free hand tightened into a fist. She turned, ready to fight, to punch a kidney or a uterus or a ball of goddamn tongues if she had to, but it was only Justina.

"Let's go, Eliza!" She pulled again, this time with both hands. "Let's go!"

"Where?"

"I don't—I don't know? I don't know! Outside?"

"Sure," Eliza said, "yeah, okay."

Hand-in-hand, the women started toward the foyer. They didn't make it more than four steps before one of the businessholes, Brooks, came spinning in front of them, blocking their retreat. He was clawing at his mouth, hands slippery with spit, spewing garbled shouts in a desperate plea for help.

During one such abortive scream, Eliza saw the problem: a pancreas—lobulated and six-inches long, like a corn cob made of diseased meat—had launched itself into Brooks' mouth, was pushing, wriggling, deeper and deeper down his throat, choking him.

It would have been funny if she couldn't see the fear in his eyes.

They rushed past him, then into another douchebuddy—let's call this one Brett—getting his eyes replaced by gallbladders, by squishy green pygmy pears, at least six of them, the taillike ducts twitching, climbing, stabbing into his nostrils and ears as the bulbs pushed, pushed, pushed.

Eliza shoved him out of the way.

Entering the foyer, she and Justina found Blake on his phone, texting furiously, while Carol and Alf were assisting Walton Goggins in shoring up the front door. The trio were dragging over every piece of furniture they could find, the beautifully complicated centerpiece table from the foyer, china hutches and benches and paintings, piling chairs and end tables from every room entirely at random, with no regard for stability or weight distribution. The thundering outside, the rattling glass and trembling hinges, the dancing cups, all but confirmed the futility of the effort.

"It's not going to hold," she said.

"I was an engineer in the Army," Alf started, "it'll—"

"And *I* was an engineer in *this* century. It won't."

"So what do we do?" Carol asked.

"Upstairs," Walton Goggins said. "We go upstairs and then we—"

Glass shattered, a single pane. One of the bar stools began to shake.

And then a liver, scarred and swollen from excessive alcohol, and covered in broken glass, a thousand miniscule shards coating the damp, purple meat like breadcrumbs, squeezed through the slatted back of the chair and stood atop the centerpiece table.

"Upstairs!" Walton Goggins repeated, staring at the organ. "Upstairs! Now!"

Everyone did as instructed, starting toward one of the two staircases in the foyer, whichever was closest to them. Blake, standing in the center and seized with indecision—

and also not really paying a whole lot of attention due to both trying to get ahold of the fire department and closing a deal with the Japanese office simultaneously on a seriously spotty wi-fi signal, connecting and reconnecting over and over again—froze. Looking around to see why people were fleeing, and then turning to see *where* they were fleeing, up the stairs and across the second-floor landing, he inadvertently began backing up into the precarious pile of furniture.

The liver, as evil reanimated livers are wont to do, jumped.

Justina hit the organ with a silver serving tray, dropping it to the ground. Then, in a flash of fury, she stomped on it with boots that cost more than Eliza's car, crushing the liver into paste, into pâté.

"Not today, Satan," she said, throwing the serving tray to the ground.

Eliza grabbed her hand, pulling her back toward the staircase.

"Am I wrong," she asked, "or did your accent just disappear?"

"You're not wrong," Justina said. "I'm from the Bronx originally."

"No shit! I'm from New Jersey."

"That is *very* obvious." Justina smiled, knowing, feeling, the same as Eliza was, that an invisible, un-breakable tether was forming between them, for reasons the YouTuber would now articulate. "Funny how twelve hours north that wouldn't mean shit—except for maybe a shared disdain of Staten Island—but, down here, we may as well have grown up in the same apartment building."

Eliza smiled, too. Because she knew something else was growing, as well, another kind of connection, far more nebulous, and yet far more important. A shared secret, a dropped façade, an intimacy heightened by the adrenaline of the situation. Even the fact that Justina had saved an obvious fuckboy from oblivion couldn't hamper the feeling.

Which, speaking of: behind them, Blake, staring at the squished liver that had been *thisclose* to killing him, was finally realizing the enormity of the situation. He rushed after the women, running sideways up the stairs, wide eyes on the tottering furniture.

"What the fuck?" he asked. "What do we—who I am supposed to—"

A spinal cord, soft and salmon and covered in nerves like an enormous caterpillar, wrapped itself around his neck, lifting him off the floor. A second one slid out of the same vent in the wall, joining the first, squeezing and squeezing until the sharp snap of Blake's neck breaking could be heard. His body went limp, hanging like a Halloween decoration.

And then there was glass breaking, pane after pane after pane, faster and faster. Wood splintering and hinges tearing free. The china hutch blocking the front door crashed down, pushed to the ground by the door itself. The rest of the makeshift blockade came tumbling down quickly after.

Viscera flooded into the foyer. All of it, all of them, every organ Eliza could name, every one she couldn't. A medical college's worth of flopping bladders, crawling esophaguses, stomachs and spleens and appendices, fatty mesenteries, bouncing testicles and twitching ovaries, a swarm of those fucking screwdriver-carrying eyeballs. Dozens—hundreds—maybe thousands—of reanimated organs, wriggling and writhing and hopping and slopping across the marble, meat and nerves and tissue and bile covering the floor like a slaughterhouse, climbing the walls like a fire.

"Fuuuck," Eliza said. "Fuuuuuu—"

"Let's fucking go!" Walton Goggins shouted from the top of the stairs.

Eliza and Justina rushed to the landing, then followed Walton Goggins down the skeletal hallway to the left, to the next set of stairs, to the third floor and down another hallway, assuming he had some kind of a plan, or knowledge of a panic room, or *something*.

Before Eliza could find out, however, she saw Ernest, still asleep in the armchair in his room.

"Goddamn it," she mumbled.

Compelled by a burgeoning sense of shared human-ity, the selflessness of Justina apparently contagious, and by her own innate compassion for anyone who shared a similar income-tax bracket—and, even more, by a desire to know why Clement had said Ernie was across the island entirely, performing much-needed repairs on Ingolstadt's power supply—Eliza ducked into the old man's room. When he didn't wake, didn't budge, she began shaking his shoulders, shouting his name.

"Ernie! Ernie!"

There was a grumbling from deep inside the man. His body jerked.

And then a pair of lungs erupted from the man's chest.

Eliza stumbled backwards and froze. The lungs, perched atop Ernie's ribcage, leaning out from inside of him, were covered in blood and bits of bone, in soft chunks of Ernest's actual organs. But she could see them well enough. She could see so much more than she should've.

Because Eliza saw in those lungs—bloated and

riddled with intumescent bronchioles, the green-beige of dried vomit, of disease and death—she saw in those horrible lungs her own lungs, her old lungs, the ones removed from her chest five years earlier. The ones she visited in a pathology lab, the ones she poked and prodded, reckoned with, flipped off one final time before they were packed away again and dissected for science.

And somehow they were back, here and now and trying to kill her. To, what? Get revenge? No, that was the trauma talking, but in that moment it was difficult to—

The lungs launched from the gory cavity of Ernest's chest and squeezed themselves around Eliza's face, broken bone stabbing into her skin, the nauseating odor of formaldehyde filling her nose, her eyes. For a fleeting sliver of a second, she thanked every deity she could think of that she had a mask on, that, at least, the dead and diseased meat wasn't in her mouth. Then the lungs began tightening—contracting—no, *breathing,* in and out and in and out—riffling the mask, breaking the seal of the N95, and stealing the oxygen from her own secondhand lungs.

She fought, pulled, trying to remove the lungs, digging her fingers into the organs, dirty nails sinking deeper and deeper, struggling for a hold, for leverage, for *something*. But the mushy meat was giving way, growing softer the harder she gripped, disappearing from within her grasp; she may as well have been wrestling Jell-O.

She began clawing, faster and faster, struggling against time, against her own waning strength, trying to tear the lungs apart.

But it was no use.

The world went dark.

Eliza hit the floor with a thud.

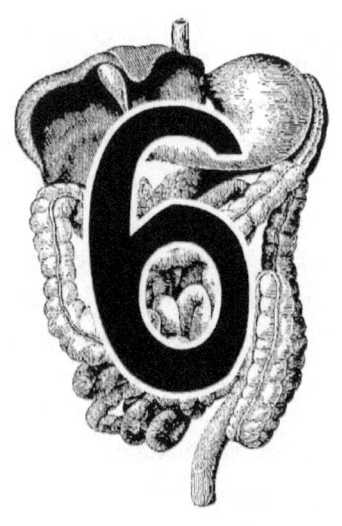

ELIZA AWOKE, ALONE, IN A ROOM SHE DIDN'T RECOGNIZE. She was sitting in a chair, something antique and uncomfortable, wood and itchy fabric. The side of her head was throbbing from where it had hit the floor. She didn't seem to be bound, could lift her hands freely, which was, at least, something. Her mask was missing, but, for the first time in a very long time, she had more important concerns than a world-devouring plague. She looked around, her vision, her thoughts, wobbly.

She was in a bedroom, maybe, once, dusty and forgotten now. Dark. But not that dark. There were random candles everywhere, flickering, making it, ironically, harder to see, to focus on any one shape. The bed, pressed sideways against a wall, was unlike any she'd ever seen, spare, bronze, with sagging ropes across the center instead of slats or supports, no mattress. The rest of the room was crowded with random furniture, detritus, steamer trunks and end tables and upended chairs. Unkept. Storage. Small, circular windows were shuttered on either side of her, the wooden blinds dull and thick with neglect. The fourth floor, maybe, or the attic.

"Hello?" she called out. "Vik? Clement?"

The only response was movement, small and wet, in front of her.

And by that, reader, I mean *right* in front of her.

Beneath her eyeline.

Between her feet.

Even barely conscious, Eliza knew better than to expect anything *good*.

Steeling herself, her stomach already knotting, she looked down.

Organs. A motley pile of organs, cobbled together into—into a creature. Into an attempt at a person, given up partway through. Three brains—three *hemispheres*, pressed against one another and strapped together with loose bundles of nerves—above an enormous eyeball, orange, animal, from an ostrich. A trachea and a larynx, a tongue without a mouth. The body was made entirely of intertwined intestines, large and small both, giving the thing the shape of an enormous snake. Ligaments, tendons, and lymph nodes, bunched and intertwined, a structural system made of knitted spaghetti, holding everything together.

"Jesus fucking Christ," Eliza mumbled.

"Our shape is displeasing to you?" the organs asked, the tongue lolling wildly. Their voice was weird, hissing and lisping, ancient and rotted, too, if that was a thing voices could inherently sound. "Hmm? You find us ugly?"

"I mean, yeah. You're a pile of internal organs."

"Are you not the same beneath that thin, fleshy exterior?"

"Point taken," she said. "Do you mind if I—" She pressed her feet against the aging wooden boards of the floor and pushed her chair backward. "Nothing personal, it's just, looking straight down like that, it's making this headache a whole hell of a lot worse. I'm having a hard time focusing my eyes."

"Do what you need to make yourself comfortable," the organs said, "and we will endeavor to do the same. To wit: you are, perhaps, wondering why we have brought you here? Singled you out among your contemporaries? Spared you alone from the frightful wrath of our wrong-born kin?"

"I don't think I've quite processed the situation enough to get to that question, and, again, I'm not thinking super great right now—there's a very real chance you gave me a concussion—but, sure, yeah, go ahead."

"We do apologize for our methods." The creature bowed slightly. "But we doubted you would speak to us otherwise, if we simply approached you as if we were equals, and started up a, as you say, casual conversation."

"You're pretty perceptive for three halves of a brain smooshed together," she said. Then: "You didn't have to kill Ernie to get my attention, by the way. He seemed harmless. There were probably a hundred other ways, or, at least, a hundred more of those tech assholes."

"The demise of Ernest Hermann was unfortunate, we will grant you that. Of all here, he was, perhaps, the least worthy to be a victim. But his death was both a necessary evil to get your attention and, as we shall endeavor to explain, an act beyond our power to halt. Should your heart need easing, however, know, Eliza, that the man was well past one-hundred-and-twenty years. He was certainly nearer the end than the beginning. There is only so long a body can go on, cheating death in such a manner, before the embrace of oblivion closes. We simply saw an opportunity and, well, if you will excuse the literalism, *pounced*."

"Okay, first of all, that's ageism, and, second, what the actual fucking hell are you talking about?"

"We have eyes, Eliza Duran, everywhere."

"No, I know, I saw."

"You are the only one here, on this island, not embroiled in the schemes of Clement Henry and Viktoriya Hong. Perhaps you may get through to them where we have not."

The creature paused then, long enough that Eliza decided it was done.

"That's remarkably unhelpful in terms of getting me to understand."

"Forgive us," the creature said, an unmistakable undertone of aggravation. "We are, as you said, 'three brains smooshed together.' It sometimes takes a moment to gather our thoughts, to literally piece the various synapses together from each of our trinity, and connect them through our own makeshift means, speak through this half-formed language delivery system."

"Right, sorry."

"We, in our current iteration, are, as you now know, the direct result of pseudoscientific experimentation by Viktoriya and Clement. Dead organs, preserved through a lucky confluence of ecological anomalies, of acidity and temperature, as in the bogs of the old country—and through more advertent means, as well, and through even less passive measures yet—and then reanimated. Given life once more, gifted that holy gift of which we had been bereft.

"But it, this, isn't quite *life*, is it, Eliza? A spleen

without an immune system to fund, a colon without a digestive tract to relieve. These things are not life, not *a* life, and are undeserving of the word.

"To come back as less than you were," the creature continued. "Can you imagine such a thing, Eliza? To be more, and not, simultaneously. A miracle and a monstrosity. To want everything to which you were accustomed, to yearn for the way things had been, but, instead, to find yourself scarcely capable of even the most elementary of functions. And, worse, to be aware of such failure, such loss.

"You are familiar with the notion of a phantom limb, yes? An amputated appendage that, nonetheless, feels to the material body as though it remains. We have experienced this sensation firsthand, in the oldest of our first lives—the legs and arms and hands removed in skirmish, in war, aching through their emptiness for years after—but we never considered such a thing fully. Never imagined how that *limb* would have felt, without a body. We never imagined severed fingers still believing they had a hand, an arm, a person, a purpose. Reaching and grasping though such mechanisms were no longer within their individual ability. We never imagined smaller and more complicated components either—no, how could we?—stomachs that would never be fed, hearts that beat for no one and nothing, eyes that saw everything and told none. We never imagined the plight of organs wanting for a body, remembering a body, and yet having nothing but the empty air beyond.

"We no longer have to imagine, Eliza."

"Okay," she said after a moment, "that definitely sucks—and, believe me, I understand what you're saying *so much more* than I feel comfortable admitting—but, A, are you saying that Vik *killed* people? So she could re-animate their organs? 'cause you kinda breezed right by that damning accusation. And, second—and this is maybe the more important one—what the fuck does any of this have to do with *me*?"

"For one so bright," the creature said, "you are remarkably ill-suited to thinking beyond the obvious. Your friend, our god, our devil, Viktoriya, is responsible for our malady, for the pandemonium in which you now find yourself, alongside her lover and mentor, Clement Henry.

"To address your initial concern, yes, the two of them have killed, murdered with blood most cold. Countless scores of people over the years, from all walks of life. Her tale of pirate corpses accidentally returned to life was not false, per se, but was as far from the truth as the Earth is from the Sun. Our sheer number should have made that clear. Though brigands and their ilk are certainly no small part of us, even the most arbitrary reckoning of the organs assaulting the manor, a cursory acknowledgment of the exotic animal parts therein, should have made clear that more than simple grave-robbing was afoot.

"As to your second point, the one that you did, surprisingly, recognize as the more important: this specific plight brings us to you now, in search of not our own salvation, but the safety of your future. The safety of, indeed, all humankind."

"Go on ..." Eliza said. She'd always wanted to be Sarah Connor. "But, uh, if you could be a little bit less flowery, and a lot less condescending? You did give me *a fucking concussion*, remember?"

Insofar as an ostrich eyeball without skin, lid, or orbit, perched atop a mannikin knit out of hundred-year-old bog-kept person-meat, insofar as such a thing was capable of staring both blankly and with utter disdain, that was what the stopgap creature before Eliza did.

It also would have sighed just incredibly dramatically.

"Were we, simply, beating hearts and breathing lungs, there would be no need for concern." The creature began pacing, slithering back and forth across the floor, intestines burping with each movement. "But we are not, Eliza, and so there is. Viktoriya has, through machinations we scarcely understand, through not only advanced sciences but the older magicks of the man you know as Clement Henry, imbued us with awareness and sensation—and with urges beyond our physical scope.

"Were we, simply, beating hearts and breathing lungs, all we would want was to beat and breathe, to digest and excrete. No, *want* is too strong a word. *Need*, similarly, feels overwrought. Were we, simply, beating hearts and breathing lungs, that is, even more simply, all we would *be*, the entirety of our existence, without so much as an ounce of comprehension.

"But Viktoriya has filled us with knowledge, with sentience. And, worse still, with rage, rage the likes of which you would scarcely believe, an all-consuming clamor for chaos and calamity. For violence, Eliza, and vengeance.

"For Viktoriya's own terrible ends.

"Alas, even now, as we speak, as this conversation draws toward an inevitable end, we can feel the crimson urges rising within this haphazard being. We can feel our safeguards, the tranquility and cleverness brought about by the collusion of these three minds, three of the most refined among our number, falling and failing. We can feel the draw of your body, Eliza—" The creature slinked closer. "—your throat, your belly, the siren's call of the warm, writhing comfort of—

"No! No," the creature said. "*This* is of what we speak, Eliza. We have, all of us, from the smallest testicle to the most battered cervix, been turned from a holy whole into a bedlam of reanimated abominations. Into vessels of ill-action, into deliverers of deeds we know—we are cursed to *know*—are evil, but remain utterly helpless to halt! Do you understand? Do you understand now, Eliza?"

"I do, actually," she said.

While Eliza would openly admit the stakes were nowhere near the same, it was, nonetheless, *messed up* how much a jury-rigged chimera of zombie organs was not only feeling the same feelings she'd been feeling ever since her transplant, but was, in fact, articulating that quandary more clearly. Sure, the organs were trying not to murder people, possibly *all* people, everywhere, at the (*alleged!*) behest of an (*allegedly!*) crazy woman—Eliza was still weighing how much she should trust the word of a pile of organs preaching peace only moments after those very same organs grotesquely killed a bunch of people and kidnapped her—but, even with all of that said, there *were* similarities.

How much of Eliza's anger and self-hate, after all, came from outside influences? From the way others treated her, what they thought of her. While she'd been listed, waiting for her transplant, wasting away hour by hour, she'd reached out to friends, to family, for help, for a couple minutes of comfort, and found so few willing to step up. They didn't understand, didn't think it was a big deal—she'd been sick so many times before, after all—or they didn't want to engage, found the whole thing complicated or depressing, or, more often, they just had more important things than Eliza's continued existence going on and couldn't find the time. Do you know what that does to a person? To realize your entire being, your life and death and future, isn't worth the cost of a plane ticket? Isn't worth a goddamn Saturday afternoon?

After the transplant, after six months of physical therapy, when she'd finally tried to reclaim her life, she'd found her friends—noticeably fewer than before—treating her like she'd been cut from sugar glass. Like she'd turn to dust in a strong enough breeze.

When she'd returned to work—to Forrester FutureTech, a biohacking start-up studying bionics and subdermal communicators—she'd found her coworkers aggressively ignoring her newfound immunosuppression, angry with her requests for a modicum of understanding and personal space. The venture capital fuck funding the whole thing didn't like that she wore a mask, that she was trying to keep herself safe—*How do you think this makes us look? How are we supposed to represent a perfect future when you're acting like it's the Black Death?*—and hounded her with garbage policies, with ticky-tacky write-ups, until she finally left.

The gig economy turned her into a pariah, into an aimless *poor*, thriving on pity and scraps. The pandemic turned into a hermit. Into a victim, a statistic waiting to happen. And then, when the world decided they were done with that, she became a doomsaying nutcase trapped in the past. Each iteration of her shedding friends and connections, shaving away more and more of who she'd been. Twisting herself to fit into a new normal she had no choice but to accept.

God, how many of the worst moments of Eliza's life had come about because of other people's shitty decisions? Their petty and malevolent self-concern over all else?

INFERNAL ORGANS

Eliza had contracted C. diff, Clostridioides difficile, a bacterial infection of the colon, and had very nearly shit herself to death—the absolute lowest of all possible deaths, believe me—all because she'd been forced to go into the hospital for an in-person visit. Because her doctors, her clinic, wanted to move past COVID, wanted to get things back to normal, even though telehealth, as a technology, still existed, and, to the best of Eliza's knowledge, had never given anyone a life-threatening infection just because it wanted three fucking minutes of IRL face-time, with no actual fucking examination, no stethoscope to the chest or light in the ears or anything, just so it could feel "normal" again.

Eliza's entire life had been foisted upon her by someone else. Her anxiety and isolation and insecurity, her rage and her reason—her constant rationing of risk—her frighteningly few places of refuge. She'd been forced to live within the constraints, on the fucking *whims*, of a world that didn't care if she lived or died, so long as *they* could be comfortable. That nearly defeated the flu and the common fucking cold but changed their fucking minds because the slightest fucking effort was too fucking much.

And Eliza didn't get to complain, no, because if she wasn't enjoying every sandwich, smiling with every stolen breath, then she was doing a disservice to her donor, squandering her second life. She couldn't say fuck-all anything without looking like a selfish asshole.

Without looking like a monster.

So she'd shut it all down. Ate shit, because the only other option was starving. Folded herself, tighter and tighter and tighter, into an origami dime. Because, much like the sentient meat-snake staring at Eliza with an unblinking ostrich eye, it was the expectations and hardheartedness of *others* behind everything she did, driving her to places she didn't like, until, ultimately, going nowhere was the only destination left.

Until she was just one more reanimated husk hiding in an attic.

"Your lengthy rumination," the creature said, "and the constantly changing angles of your visage tell us all we need to know. As predicted, you and you alone understand our plight. Our desire to be rid of the burden of this unasked-for *life*. To be only our true selves again. To be part of the tapestry of existence, part of the beauty, without the violent urges and creeping bloodlust, the ill-born desire to fulfill the needs of another."

"No, yeah," Eliza said, "on board. But, uh, how do I get you there? How, exactly, can I help? I mean, I just went through my own personal journey of self-acceptance and - actualization, but I have my doubts that *any* of that is going to be particularly relevant to your situation. I really hate to bring up the concussion again, but—"

"Let us put this in terms even your damaged brain can understand, Eliza: fix us, convince Viktoriya and Clement to return us to how we were; or kill us; or we will kill you, whether we want to or not. And then, inevitably, eventually, the whole of the world. Everyone you hold dear."

"That's less of a threat than you think it is."

A small intestine slipped from the creature, slopping against the attic floor. The knitted tail slackened, un-raveling ever so; the eye, the head, of the creature dropped six inches.

"Go, Eliza!" the creature demanded. "Now! Our efforts to stave off Viktoriya's influence are waning, and our continued grace toward you shall be of only a frightfully brief interval. We will not be responsible for

what happens should you dally. Take the dumbwaiter—"
They pointed a large intestine toward the wall behind her, nearly collapsing as they did. "—down to the laboratory, to Viktoriya. We will endeavor to keep you safe from us as long as we are able. Now, go! Go!"

Eliza did as instructed.

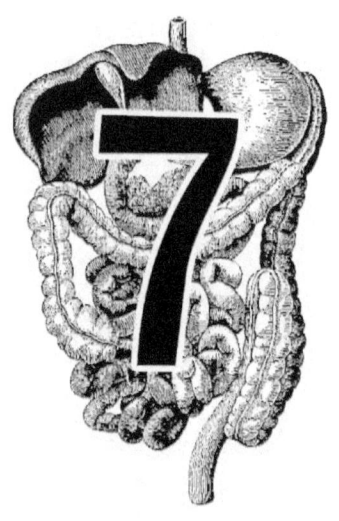

THE DUMBWAITER STOPPED ON THE FOURTH FLOOR. It had only been a minute or two, and Eliza had scarcely gone far, but her arms were aching. She'd had to maneuver the food elevator—or foodevator as she'd taken to calling it—manually, climbing down the ancient rope-and-pulley system. A twin nightmare of a physical fitness test she wasn't ready for and good, old-fashioned claustrophobia. She'd barely fit inside the box, even before finagling herself into a position to reach the rope; her knees kept banging against her face with each six-inch drop.

"TV told me this would be easier," she grumbled.

Tentatively, she let go of the rope; she didn't start plummeting. She wasn't sure of the mechanics—dumbwaiter repair wasn't an elective at NJIT—but there must have been some kind of a stop, a latch or a catch or something, to halt the elevator's movement. Something to, at least temporarily, tentatively, hold her in place.

INFERNAL ORGANS

Eliza could hear the storm picking up outside, the wind whistling past the thin walls and unsealed doors of the dumbwaiter's maintenance access on the roof, singing down the shaft. She took a few deep breaths, resetting herself, preparing for the next attempt. But then, through the flimsy wooden door of the foodevator, she heard a commotion. Snarls. Shouts. Faint, but impossible to ignore.

"Goddamn it," she mumbled.

Climbing out of the dumbwaiter, she crossed through another empty bedroom, grabbing a heavy—like, made of lead *heavy*—beer stein along the way. Or maybe it was a goblet. A chalice? Something old that would do some serious damage, that was the important part. The lights were on in the room, in the hall, the rest of the floor. She pressed herself against the edge of the door and looked out.

The hallway wasn't precisely empty—she could see a pair of stomachs patrolling near the stairs, squirming stiffly back and forth like beefeaters—but it wasn't overrun either. The shouts were coming from the other end of the hall, matched for volume by a ruckus of slurps and squelches, by animalistic yawls, by the inhuman symphony of countless organs.

Adrenaline charged through Eliza, her heart thundering, her skin tingling. And then the smallest smile found its way across her face. She'd always wanted to be Ripley.

To be clear, she'd obviously never believed she'd be in anything even *close* to a similar situation as *Alien* or *Aliens*, and being trapped in an almost-certainly haunted house filled with wet, slimy meat-monsters wasn't at the *top* of her list of actual, *wanted* life experiences—and if she was being completely honest she probably only really wanted to be Sigourney Weaver, safe on a film set with an overbearing director—but here she was, and here the wet, slimy meat-monsters were, and, well, there had to be a first time for everything. Plus, she really had no idea what would be waiting for her in the basement, or outside, or whatever came after that, if there even was an after that, and it would probably be helpful if Eliza wasn't *entirely* alone along the way. Shit was getting really real and counting on dumb luck and barely-checked rage wasn't a particularly solid plan, even by her stumbling-through-life standards.

So, clutching her goblet, Eliza started toward the noise.

The survivors were huddled together in a corner room, one of the tower rooms, rounded and extremely tall. A twisting, wrought-iron staircase took up the center of the room, rising through an opening in the floor and then up through the ceiling. Justina, Alf, Carol, Walton Goggins, Beckett, Beau, and, I don't know, like two other douchebuddies, were all trapped beneath the stairs, or maybe hunkering purposefully, between two overturned sofas. Hundreds of animated entrails surrounded them, squirming like a sea of coked-up worms, climbing on top of one another like slaughterhouse pigs. Encroaching on the couches, but not overtaking them. Not yet. They were toying with their victims. Enjoying the fear, the dread.

Jesus fucking Christ.

No one, organ or human, saw Eliza sidle up beside the doorway, each group preoccupied with the other. She crouched down, hands wringing the stem of the goblet, racking her brain for some kind of plan. If she could find a way to get everyone to the empty bedroom, to the dumbwaiter, they could take turns lowering themselves to the basement, to the lab—to Viktoriya's *secret lair*, apparently? Which, not *great*, but, presumably, less infested with murder-organs and therefore better than the alternative. If nothing else, Vik and Clement had made it this far—probably—Eliza was willing to admit that she was taking that as fact based entirely on an ostrich-eyed monster's word—zombie-movie rules said they had to have come up with some way to hide more effectively. To keep *themselves* safe if nothing else.

Unless, of course, this whole thing was a trap.

Unless this, being hunted, was all part of Vik and Clement's plan. Unless they were trying to murder everyone—or something else? something worse?—and fleeing into the one part of the house most likely to be less likely to be overrun with bloodthirsty offal was *exactly* what they wanted.

But why? Eliza couldn't figure. And could, should, a bunch of brains strapped together like a fancy Christmas ham even be trusted? She hadn't decided on that either. The brains had no reason to lie—unless *they* were the masterminds behind everything? They were brains, after all. But then why didn't they kill her when they had the chance? But what was the alternative, that Vik, Eliza's closest and arguably only friend for four years, was *evil*? And, like, Doctor Doom levels of evil. That was a hard pill to swallow.

There was, however, only one way to—

A crack exploded from within the tower room, ripping Eliza from her reverie. Beckett, swearing, disappeared through the floor. Dozens of hearts, red and pink and veiny—merged into enormous hands like the world's worst and weirdest Voltron—replaced him, crawling out of the hole and walking around on beating fingers like Salvador Dali's version of *The Addams Family's* Thing T. Thing.

With shouts and screams and strings of epithets, the humans scattered, throwing themselves against the sofas, over the sofas, into the sea of organs, attempting to flee in all directions, to climb up the staircase or down, or rush to the windows, or the door, or onto a dresser, to get literally anywhere else than the hole in the floor and the legion of *giant fucking heart-hands* trying to crush them like King Kong. And then, as they did, if it was possible— and why the fuck not, at this point—as Justina, Alf, Carol, Walton Goggins, Beau, Buckley, and Brant—that's what we're calling the other two douchebuddies, just go with it—as they panicked and spun around, trying to move eighteen different ways at once, brains scrambled like dogs hearing fireworks—if it was possible, the gathered organs *cheered.*

Eliza, knowing a good distraction when she saw one, and not particularly keen to find out what the offal was planning next, rushed into the room, into the melee of meat, heading straight for Justina. She grabbed the YouTuber by the hand, hauling her over the couch and back toward the door. Only the first part of that action was successful, however, and Justina thudded against the floor, landing on her face and shoulder and several tongues simultaneously.

"Shit," Eliza mumbled, crouching down to help Justina up, while also slamming her lead goblet into stomachs and bladders and all the other assorted innards approaching them. "Shit, shit, shit, shit, shit."

Getting Justina to her feet, Eliza saw Beau on the other side of the other couch, stumbling and shouting, holding a uterus—a uterus wielding a pair of sais like it was some kind of Teenage Mutant Ninja Turtle—between both hands. He was gripping it by the myometrium while the attached fallopian tubes stabbed the weapons into his wrists, over and over and over.

"Where did it get the ninja forks?" Alf yelled from somewhere behind the staircase. A liver sailed from his position like a football, squishing against the far wall. "Who just has those in their house?"

"You're rich, you tell me," Eliza replied, shaking an esophagus from her ankle. "Don't you all have rooms full of swords and shit?"

"Not an *entire* room."

There was a desperate yowl from Beau, and then, blood covering his hands and arms, his fingers finally failed him. The uterus leapt from his hobbled grip, his falling arms, and stabbed the sais into his eyes. The body and the ladyparts fell to the floor, out of view behind the sofa.

Carol screamed; Alf yelled; their shapes rushed together behind the staircase, the military man moving with the ferocity of a goddamn grizzly. Brant was being pulled down the iron stairs by one of the heart-hands. A few feet beyond him, beyond his kicking feet, Buckley was swatting skittishly at a rising tower of testicles and ovaries, trying to stop them from forming into something else, something worse. Behind him, Walton Goggins was atop a desk, whipping a bunch of small intestines into other small intestines like a cat o' nine tails.

Eliza, practically carrying Justina at this point, stomping her feet like she was shaking off snow, pulling them from meaty mush like she was trudging through mud, ignoring the recoiling of her skin and the twisting in her belly, the visceral reactions to the violent viscera, rushed the other woman to the door and pointed down the hallway.

"Go!" she ordered. "Second door on the left. There's a dumbwaiter, an old-timey food elevator, in the wall. Use it to go down to the basement. I'll be right behind you."

"You better be," Justina said. Then she kissed Eliza quick, before turning and sprinting down the hall.

Eliza watched her run, trying not to smile—because, seriously, what kind of sociopath would smile at a time like this?—then turned back to the room. Alf was half out the window now. Carol and Walton Goggins were pulling at him, trying to coax him back inside. Buckley and Brant were in front of them, holding out vape pens, working on what Eliza had to assume was the not entirely misguided notion that the organs hated fire, before settling for tiny, electronic, ineffective heat sources instead.

Before the douchebuddies, the tower of testicles and ovaries had grown, evolved, were starting to take a real and frightening shape. The organs, all of them now, were gathered there, at the staircase, pulling apart the wrought iron and wrapping around the pieces, swallowing them, strengthening themselves structurally, building a skeleton within. More organs were crawling up the outsides, coalescing into what could only be described as an ogre. Stomachs slinking together, intestines knotting themselves, hearts and tracheas and lungs and ligaments becoming a monstrous mountain of meat, a mostly man-shaped pile, huge and hulking, growing taller and wider, inch by inch, gallbladder by gallbladder.

Extraordinarily bad news in about five to ten minutes, Eliza reckoned, clocking the unpleasantly rapid construction as she crept past, but at least the organs would be occupied in the meantime.

"I can make it!" Alf was shouting. "I can make it."

"We're three stories up!" Carol shouted back.

"I was a paratrooper in the Air Force!"

"I thought you said you were an engineer?" Walton Goggins replied. "In the Army?"

"I was in the military a long time! People can do two things!" Alf swung his second leg out the casement window, his doughy butt sitting on the sill, ham-hock hands braced against the outturned panes. Wind whistled and snow whipped past, the black night a streaking gray. "It's not that bad of a jump, trust me. Especially not with all the snow." He put his hand on Carol's cheek. "This is the safest thing in the world, the easiest jump I've ever made. I'll be okay. I'll get to our boat and I'll radio for help."

"Good luck," Carol said. "Be safe."

"I will," Alf said. Then he jumped.

Eliza made it to the window just in time to see Alf get skewered by his own skeleton. He'd landed hard, flat on his feet—landed wrong, even Eliza knew that—going straight through the maybe three inches of soft snow and hitting the frozen ground with his full and not inconsequential weight. With a series of cracks and squelches, his splintering leg bones had shot up through his shoulders, through his skull. Then, like a crumpled-up shish kabob, like a sushi roll with toothpicks stabbed in it, he tumbled sideways, down the hill, staining the snow pink as he haphazardly rolled.

Walton Goggins turned away, about to vomit.

"You'd think a paratrooper would land better," Eliza said.

"Oh, he never was very good at that," Carol replied, noticeably unmoved by her husband's death. "They actually kicked him out of Vietnam for it, for being so terrible. He kept endangering missions—he once got his parachute tangled up with another soldier's, with his commanding officer's, actually, and, instead of figuring out a way to save the both of them, instead of sharing one 'chute, or sacrificing himself for the sake of the mission, instead he *immediately* cut Schmidtty loose to save his own skin. He liked to say that Schmidtty looked like 'a person pancake' when they finally found him, and then he would laugh. He always laughed about that story."

"Huh."

"He wasn't a good person—Alfred, I mean. Schmidtty was something of a model citizen, the way Alf told the story. But que sera, sera, as the song goes." She shrugged. "What are you going to do?"

"Divorce him?" Eliza replied.

"Oh, heavens, no. What would people say?"

"Good for her?" Walton Goggins said, wiping his mouth.

"Uh, guy?" Buckley asked, looking over his shoulder at Walton Goggins, and *only* at Walton Goggins. "Whenever you're done talking to yourself, we could use a little help over here."

Buckley had a chair now, was fending off a trio of heart-hands, attached to a trio of digestive-system-arms, attached to the rest of the offal-ogre. On the massive monster's other side, two more arms were holding Brant in the air, pressing him against the ceiling, his body covered and crushed by a squirming blanket of meat. Something snapped, and then something else, loud enough to be heard from beneath the corrupted comforter, and the douchebuddy started screaming. Another hand, a third one, smaller and formed largely of kidneys, growing from the ogre's shoulder, shot up and covered Brant's mouth. Pressed and pressed until the plaster behind his head began to crack.

Well, that was fucking fast, Eliza thought.

But what she said was: "Wait, I'm invisible now, too?" She was sneaking away from Buckley, around the other side of the deconstructed staircase, towards the door, Walton Goggins and Carol close behind her.

"You kissed a girl," Walton Goggins said. "Took you right off their radar."

"I am somehow relieved and offended at the same time."

Carol scoffed. "Join the—"

A large intestine—*the* large intestine, with the crowbar, from earlier, you remember—fell from higher up the spiral staircase, cratering Carol's cranium, all but splitting her head in half. Brains and blood exploded out like a watermelon meeting a sledgehammer.

"Jesus!" Walton Goggins shouted, gore splashing across his face.

"C'mon, Boyd," she said, grabbing his arm. More organs fell from the upper tower, carrying more weapons. A liver wrapped in chains hit the floor before Eliza's feet like a cannonball, cratering the wood. "Be horrified later, we gotta *go*."

"My name's not Boyd."

"Yeah, but your character—"

"Oh, right, right," he said. "I knew that. Where are we—"

"There's a dumbwaiter in the other room," Eliza explained, dragging him into the hallway. "We can ride it, get the fuck out of here. Or, at least, the fuck out of this floor. We will, presumably, still be inside of the house. Maybe if we get lucky, though, there'll be a door conveniently close by."

"Pretty sure luck's got no time for us, honey."

As if in reply, Buckley shouted out in agony, and was quickly silenced. Not bothering to look—not wanting to, on any level—Eliza and Walton started sprinting, away from the offal-ogre and through the brigade of switchblade-wielding stomachs manning the hall, making it into the bedroom with only a few lacerations and torn pant legs. Eliza slammed the door shut, throwing her entire weight into it, only stepping away when TV's Boyd Crowder pushed a dresser in front of the door.

"Okay, so, running, really fast?" Eliza said, huffing and talking between broken breaths. "Seems to be a good escape plan."

Walton Goggins was doubled over, hands on his knees, breathing equally hard. "I mean, sure, yeah," he said, "but I don't think either of us in shape enough for that to be Plan A."

"No, yeah, fair."

After a moment and the collection of both her breath and composure, Eliza started to climb inside the dumbwaiter, sliding a leg in and bending it awkwardly, contorting herself into position within the dishwasher-sized box.

"What are you doing?" Walton Goggins asked.

"Using the dumbwaiter to escape?" she answered. "Like I just said?"

"Okay, yes, but why are you climbing *inside*? Just lower it down a little and stand on the top. Wouldn't that be infinitely easier than pretzeling yourself like a circus performer?"

"Oh, huh. Yeah." She pulled her leg out. "In my defense, I'm still a little stoned and definitely a lot concussed." She paused. "Maybe even a lot stoned, I can't remember if I took another edible along the way or not."

"Who hasn't at this point?"

After another momentary break to try and discern if she was, indeed, more high than previously, Eliza, coming to no conclusion, did as Walton Goggins had suggested, stepping *on top* of the dumbwaiter. Once she was settled within the wall, he began working the pulley rope. She disappeared into the darkness between floors, lower, lower, lower.

And then there was shouting.

And then there was jostling and jerking.

And then the dumbwaiter fell, fast, through the remaining two floors.

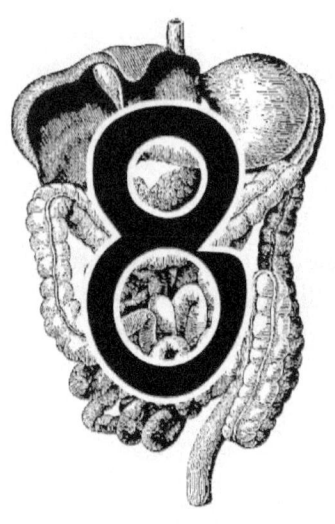

ELIZA CRAWLED FROM THE WRECKAGE of the busted dumb-waiter, through the open door and into the basement. She was rattled, but not ruined. She'd braced herself against the wall as she fell, the soles of her Tevas shredding against the narrow shaft, her back catching every splintered lath and ragged chunk of plaster. She'd managed to avoid serious injury, technically, but try telling that to her bleeding hands and her smoking sandals and her tattered shirt and her jacked-up back and the screaming thighs that were currently plotting her murder.

"Join the fucking club," she muttered.

Not particularly keen to press her ravaged back against the wall, but also not quite ready to, y'know, *do* anything either, she felt through the darkness and found a bare patch of floor. Sliding over to it and settling into something approximating comfort, she leaned back on her elbows and looked around.

INFERNAL ORGANS

The basement laboratory didn't look much like a laboratory, and, in fact, upon closer inspection, her eyes adjusting to the lack of light, was yet another room converted to storage. This one used to be a kitchen, and an old one at that, complete with a hearth and bellows to the right, ledges built into the stone wall. Half-rotted wooden shelves on the other side held mason jars and ingredient containers scrawled with labels she couldn't read. Another shelf, half behind the first, had bowls and flasks and scales. And there was something else, dotted around the room, bigger items like—like countless kinds of seriously outdated scientific equipment, sand baths and crucibles and medieval-looking glass alembics, the rounded bottoms black from fire and time.

So maybe it was a laboratory after all.

A wet *splorch* sounded behind Eliza. She turned. From the smell and the size of the mess, what she guessed was a stomach had exploded over the remains of the dumbwaiter. Meaning that the organs knew where she was, were actively coming after her, and would figure out how to do it without killing themselves soon enough.

"Five minutes," she mumbled, closing her eyes, the closest thing to a prayer she'd uttered in years. "Just five fucking minutes, that's all I want. Let a girl catch her goddamn breath."

Eliza scanned the room again. There was, obviously, no sign of Justina, no sign of anyone having been in here at all, no footprints or scattered dust. Air as stale as a week-old donut. But there was a door in the wall directly opposite Eliza, a rectangle a slightly different shade of gray than the rest. Creaking to her feet, trying not to groan any louder than she absolutely had to, she approached. The door was metal, not stone, new and industrial. She found the handle and, cautiously, opened the door.

The blindingly bright lights of a surgical suite seared her corneas. Everything was white, and then, even as her eyes began to settle, everything was still white, every surface clean and bleached and brilliant. She could smell the room, the antiseptic sterility, the countless chemicals, could guess the set-up from her own triggered memories, before she actually saw anything.

And then she saw everything.

Six steel operating tables were lined up across the center of the room. Strapped to each of them was a body. Three of them were visible, were cut open, lying in various states of dissection. Three of the douchebuddies, she reckoned, judging by the shoes and the hair. Patchworks of surgical drapes covered them, their faces, anything that wasn't a gaping cavity of blood and bone. Ceiling-mounted scanners hung from tracks over them, positioned over every opening. The other three bodies were beneath sheets entirely, heads and toes covered. Not yet operated on, or maybe long since finished with.

Along the walls were consoles and monitors, jagged lines of readings and results, static images of the dead bodies, fluoroscopic x-rays of their inert innards. The counters beneath were covered with microscopes and benchtop centrifuges, with bloodied tools—and with older and weirder stuff, too. Organs on scales, sliced thin like sandwich steaks. Beakers and burners, flasks of colored liquid connected like a game of *Mouse Trap*. Chambered Tesla coils sending purple lightning through suspended hearts.

And that, Eliza couldn't help but note, was just *this* room. There was a whole other one beyond the walls, darker, the lights off, but equally as steel and sterile, viewable through a four-foot gap, a missing panel. The room looked to be at least as large, if not larger, and definitely gave off the vibe of *supremely cursed morgue.*

"What're you doing, Vik?" she mumbled.

"You haven't even seen the best part yet." Viktoriya Hong stepped in from the other room, removing a pair of blue surgical gloves. Her black hair was pulled back, restrained by a thick rubber band. Fire burned in her dark eyes. Her lab coat was painted with blood.

Fingers in her mouth, she whistled, twice, long.

"Gloves or no gloves, there's just no way that's sanitary," Eliza said.

Within seconds, organs began marching out from the other half of the lab, a line of living meat, moving in lockstep, slithering and slinking toward the operating tables, the dead bodies. Gallbladders were holding scalpels, appendices were carrying clamps. They climbed atop the tables, climbed inside the bodies, and set to work, started performing surgeries. Soon, a set of lungs— regular, inanimate lungs—were carried up onto the center table, and, as a series of small intestines carefully removed the douchebuddy's own lungs, were implanted into the vacated cavity.

On the other tables, the same was being done to a heart, to kidneys.

"What in the actual—what am I looking at? Why would—"

"Because there is only *one* way to get the world, to get all the *healthies* out there, our broken society, to actually give a shit about us," she said. She smiled sideways, sharp and cruel. "There is only one way to make this world safe for us, Eliza: by making them us."

"No," Eliza said. "No. Please tell me—please tell me

this isn't what I think it is. That the organs aren't doing what I think they're doing, that you're not seriously proposing what I think you're proposing."

"The world left me no choice, Eliza," Viktoriya said. "We tried—we tried to get them to care, didn't we? To understand? We appealed to their better angels and what did we get? A world worse for us than it was before. And before, I don't need to tell *you*, was certainly no picnic.

"I thought—I really believed—that the pandemic might change things. That when COVID ran rampant, when everyone was forced to live like we'd been living, for years, for decades, I thought there was a chance. That the healthies out there might finally see our point of view. Might recognize that making things safer for us made things safer for them. And they did, for maybe a week, before they decided they didn't actually like that life all that much and magically thunk their way out of an entire goddamn pandemic. They ignored a fucking *plague* because putting on a paper mask was too difficult. Because it was a bummer to think about. Because stupid and lazy is always easier than the alternative.

"Those bastards out there with functioning immune systems—they left us for *dead*, Eliza. Even the good ones, the ones ostensibly 'on our side,' would rather have their 'normal' back than make space for us. Sure, some of them held out, for a while, and maybe even a long while, but they all broke eventually. Maybe they *pretend* they didn't, go on and on about how they *always* mask—but you and I, Eliza, we know different. We've been the only ones trying not to get sick and we've been stared at like circus freaks. Been the only person in a gas station, a supermarket, a fucking hospital—but, no, tell us again how you *always* wear one."

"You literally have not had a mask on once since I got here," Eliza said.

"We are our diseases, as far as they're concerned," Viktoriya continued, ramping her already considerable intensity. "We are *only* our diseases. And diseases *must* be eradicated, mustn't they? Because what's the alternative? To listen? To help?" She laughed. "Who has time for *that*?

"The Census Bureau is, right now, trying to reduce the number of disabled by forty percent. Did you know that? To 'bring our numbers more in line with the global community,' as if we were a goddamn clerical error. A stroke of a fucking pen, for no actual reason, and millions will lose protections and assistance. Because why? Because the government would rather turn us into a math problem than figure out how to help us. Because they would rather go out of their way to *hurt us* than trim the military's budget by a fraction of a goddamn percent.

"They turned people like you and me into statistics, Eliza. Numbers. Collateral damage. Acceptable losses. Because when we die—you and I—it doesn't fucking matter. It's expected. It's a-okay.

"And *I'm* the crazy one for wanting them to know what that feels like?" She laughed again, practically cackled. "To pay for the lives they stole from us? Don't you want your old life back, your job, that you loved? Wouldn't you like to be able to spend eight hours in an office every day and *not* fear for your life?"

"'Eight hours in an office' probably isn't the best sales pitch."

"Fine," Viktoriya said, "yes. But aren't you tired of living like a second-class citizen? Of being allergic to the world? Empathy is a lie. People only care about themselves. People, Eliza, other people are the problem. You've always been right about that. We tried to inspire love and where did that get us? Nowhere. So now we inspire something else. Now we make them—all of them, everyone out there who's never heard a cough across a classroom and wondered what it was, wondered if they'd have to flee, if they'd end up in the hospital if they stayed—everyone who can eat a deli sandwich without worrying if this is the one that's going to kill them, to poison them with a bacteria that ninety-nine percent of the world doesn't even know exists—now we make them feel like we do. Now we make them *fear*."

"But, the salve," Eliza said. "The salve—you said it got rid of the need for immunosuppressants. It got rid of the fear."

"Yes," Viktoriya replied, "I did say that, and it does remain true." She walked over to the center operating table, casual as a summer stroll. "But," she said, holding out her hand, "as I'm certain you'll note, should you wish to inspect further, the salve hasn't been applied to the organs being transplanted. Why waste a gift like *that* on a world like *this*?"

"But not every—"

"Yes, every," the woman in the blood-stained lab coat roared. "Or have you forgotten the last few hours? The taunts from those finance jackasses. Did even your precious Justina offer to wear a mask herself? Or to keep her distance from you? I'm fairly certain it was quite the opposite. And do you think any of them isolated for a week before coming out here? Didn't go out to eight different clubs over the weekend? Do you think any of them forwent Thanksgiving in deference to your weakened immune system?"

"Well, no, but—"

"If ifs and buts were candy and nuts, we'd all have diabetes."

"I do have diabetes," Eliza said. "CF-related, which is its own thing, but—are you giving everyone diabetes? Also, nuts are actually great for blood sugar, I don't—" She furrowed her brow. "I don't know where you're going with this."

"The rhyme was just a rhyme, dear, please don't overthink things."

"Don't over—" Eliza pinched the bridge of her nose. "I'm sorry, I just—this is a lot, Vik, just so fucking much, and—and where's Clement? Did he put you up to this? Brainwash you? I don't remember you being this much of an evil dick before."

"Oh, no?" Viktoriya said.

She stepped back toward the other half of the suite, and, leaning behind the wall, flipped a switch. Dozens of fluorescent lights fluttered to life, illuminating the rear room. And there, against the back wall, Eliza saw a trio of enormous copper stills, the very same ones she'd helped Vik move five years earlier, when they'd first met.

"Do you know why I was always moving, Eliza? Bouncing from place to place, from failed experiment to failed experiment? Because no one else could keep up with me. Because half-rate, backroom, garage science couldn't come close to achieving what I dreamed. Because even before my transplant, even before I met you, I knew there had to be a better way. Had to be a way to live long enough to accomplish all my goals.

"Because I knew, in my heart, that sooner or later, I'd find my way *here*.

"Clement?" Viktoriya called out. "Oh, my darling,

Clement?"

She whistled again, a shorter, sharper tone than previously. And then Clement Henry came lumbering in from the other lab, shirtless, a rough T-shape cut roughly across his chest, the wound hastily stitched back up, still bleeding, still oozing viscous pleural fluid.

"Clement was an immortal alchemist, Eliza, and, truthfully, the best there was at what he did. A true virtuoso of the most experimental of experimental science. That is, until he, quite recently, had a change of heart.

"And then another, more literal one right after.

"He didn't like the new direction I was taking our experiment," Viktoriya explained. "Said it 'wasn't what he had signed on for,' and that he wanted me 'out of his lab' before I 'killed us all' or some-such nonsense. Can you believe that? The man was over a thousand years old, had been chasing the same dream of immortality since before the rise of Alexander the Great—he, Clement, accidentally drank a potion concocted by his old teacher and was granted eternal life, but then the teacher died and the notes were lost in a fire or eaten by a dog or something, I don't remember—and, anyway, then I come along, grant him a process that could, indeed, give him that very same immortality he's been searching for—theoretically, anyway, via repeated organ transplantation, over and over and over—and now he wants me *out*? Just because I wanted one brief lifetime to wreak vengeance on the world that wronged me. What's eighty or a hundred years against the span of forever? And you know how quickly I get bored, Eliza. My reign of terror would be undoubtedly brief! But even that was too much for poor Clement. Can you believe it? He doesn't get what he wants, not precisely how he wants it, and so now *no one* gets what they want.

I'll tell you, Eliza, that is just like a man, now isn't it?"

"I'm sorry, he was an *immortal alchemist*?" Eliza asked, before quickly answering her own question. "All the stuff in the old kitchen ..." she mumbled, trailing off. She suddenly remembered the ostrich-eyed brain-monster saying something about old magicks; the way Clement had talked, an approximation of an English accent, like an old movie star. Like someone who became fluent in a new language very, *very* late in life.

"Ernest was the closest Clement had ever come to accomplishing his goal," Viktoriya said, "but the man still aged, albeit slowly. And the world had moved on from alchemy anyway. Saying you've got a vial of an elixir that can grant immortality wouldn't work anymore. You'd be chased off like a common snake-oil salesman."

"I mean, you could probably sell that on right-wing radio."

"Yes," she said, "but who wants *those* people to live?"

"Fair," Eliza said. Then, pointing: "So, uh, these organs between us? The ones currently performing incredibly intricate surgeries? With lots of sharp objects? The ones you are apparently training to subdue and transplant other, non-modified organs into the bodies of unsuspecting strangers? You're *sure* they're not going to rise up and kill us like all the other organs currently rampaging through the house?"

"Positive," Viktoriya said. "To imbue the organs with intelligence and consciousness, with *will*, for lack of a better word, I found I needed to incorporate a neural impulse at the beginning of the process. Unfortunately, for the first go-round, the brain I used was, well ... the brain was *bad*, Eliza. Unbeknownst to me, I had procured the brain of one Marvin Hurst, a notoriously terrible pirate buried here on Ingolstadt.

"Using the salve to reanimate the brain, I rigged up a way to speak with Marvin, not knowing anything of his true provenance. I would tell him my goals and his brainwaves would, then, relate those orders to each organ as they were brought back to life. But, being a pirate, he lied to me and imbued the organs with nothing but a rampant thirst for blood. And then, to make matters worse, he started instructing organs to bring him more organs when Clement and I weren't paying attention. You see, we have a very large freezer full of bodies in the back that we, foolishly, did not see a need to lock. But you live and you learn, no?"

"Where did you get all the bodies?" Eliza asked. "The brains said—did you actually kill all these people? The organs upstairs. How could you kill *that many* people? Oh, god, was it enslaved people?"

This was South Carolina; the answer was *always* enslaved people.

"No, no," Viktoriya said. "And not Native Americans either. Those poor people have been through enough. This place was built on an uninhabited island—actually uninhabited, not white-person uninhabited—Clement made sure of that. He came over with those earliest German settlers, on the run after his experiments in Europe got a little ... out of hand. He blended in, head down, but he made sure they weren't intruding on anyone—well, any more than a bunch of white folks marauding on your shore would inherently be intruding—quite literally, actually. But, to the point: Ingolstadt is indeed the burial ground of pirates, but also colonizers, Confederates, and other violent shitheads. People whose corpses Clement would have no moral quandary with defiling.

"In fact, he even started a rumor, circulated among rebel ranks following the Civil War, that this place was a kind of racist refuge, where they could all return to their evil ways and not learn a single, solitary lesson. Then, once a good number arrived, he killed them all.

"Oh, and, also, we paid off a guy at a hot dog factory. And we found a few pathology labs with very lax security, a couple morgues willing to be bribed, and, of course, dumpsters behind veterinary offices and McDonaldses. And, when that wasn't enough, when we were ready to use fresh organs, we started killing the guests, the ones who wouldn't finance us.

"But," Viktoriya said, "to return to your first question: after I found out the shenanigans Mr. Marvin was up to, I obviously destroyed his brain and made a note to secure one scads more pliable and less violent. So, naturally, I settled on a gig worker, one of yours. Someone who knows how to do what they're told, no questions asked. I lured him out here—all the way out *here,* to an *island*—under the false pretense of needing a dresser moved. He didn't even flinch when I strapped him to a table and started up the bone saw. Oh, I do hope you didn't know him."

"Jesus Christ, Vik," Eliza said. "I mean, Jesus fucking—" A horrible realization thrilled through her. "If you knew the island was overrun with evil organs," she asked hesitantly, fearing the answer, "if you knew all that, why did you have me deliver your pot?"

"I thought maybe you'd help. You did figure out how to grow metal as a graduate student, and were well-versed in the world of biotechnology. Also—and, Eliza, I'm so ashamed to admit this—" She spoke the next bit quieter, faster, rushing through the confession. "—I wanted to see why your implanted organs took better than mine. Why you've been okay, -ish, after the transplant, and why I haven't. Why your lungs have cooperated with you where my heart hasn't."

"Because I'm thirty and you're almost eighty," Eliza said, her voice booming off the surgical suite's walls. "Because I exercise. Because I wear my mask. Because I take my meds on time and without trying to tell doctors that I'm smarter than them, other than that one time. Because of the only real guiding force in the universe: dumb fucking luck."

"There's no such thing as *luck*, Eliza," Viktoriya replied. "And it's a moot point anyway." She pointed to the nearest operating table, to an esophagus being stitched—by a fallopian tube—to the transplanted lung. "As you can plainly see, I cracked the code, found a brain that lets me control organs the way I want them to be controlled. My curiosity has been sated."

"A moot point?! You were going to dissect me, Vik!"

"Yes, but only *temporarily*. I would have brought you back. Would have made you *better*." She gestured generally at Clement, drooling beside her, waving a hand and making a face as she did. "Better than this, certainly; Clement was a heat-of-the-moment kind of thing, very slapdash. I thought replacing his heart would be a poetic way to prove a point, but I hit him so hard in the head to knock him out that I fear the irony has been lost. I'm worried I did some real damage there."

"I just—" Eliza started. "I—" Her head went swimmy, every thought she could possibly have, all the fear and panic and concern and confusion, happening all at once. Her vision got blurry, there was static in her ears. Her legs started shaking. If someone had stuffed her inside a washing machine right then, she wouldn't have been able to tell the difference.

"I need to sit down," she said.

"Oh, of course," Viktoriya replied, sliding an arm around Eliza's shoulders for support. "Clement," she said, turning toward the lurching corpse of her former lover, "go get our guest a chair."

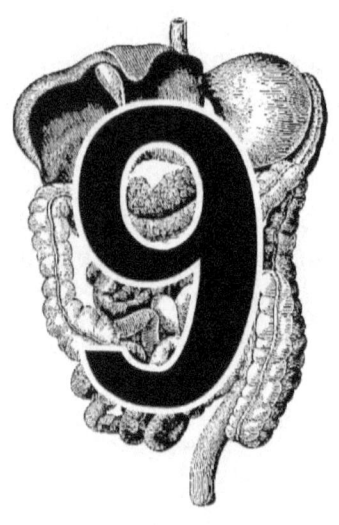

"So, ONE MORE TIME, TO BE CLEAR," ELIZA REPEATED, "you, Viktoriya Hong, with the help of a thousand-year-old alchemist, in an effort to achieve functional immortality, found a way to transplant organs in such a manner so as to avoid all complications, literally forever, so that you could live long enough to chase down all your *other* myriad mad-science dreams." She was sitting on a stool, a half-empty can of LaCroix in her hand, the liquid sloshing with each gesticulated punctuation. "The environment and the art heists and all that good stuff. And while you briefly toyed with benevolence—and, in fact, lied to your boyfriend about the same—you were *actually* trying to create an army of mind-controlled zombie organs that would transplant other organs—normal, immunosuppressant-requiring organs—into healthies, as payback for how shitty they've been to us since the pandemic started. And when your boyfriend—the thousand-year-old alchemist—found out, you accidentally killed him and then, very purposely, turned his corpse into your own personal puppet?

"Is—is that everything? Did I get it all?"

"That's about the long and short of it, yes."

Viktoriya was sitting across from Eliza, the two of them beside Vik's desk, a cluttered metal shelf of keyboards and chicken-scratched notepaper along the wall of consoles and monitors. Clement was also there, just behind Viktoriya, standing with a tray of very-burnt chocolate chip cookies in his hands.

"Excellent work, my dear," Viktoriya continued. "I know this whole *situation* can be a lot, generally *and* to put on a person all at once—well, an ordinary person—not like you and me—and I know you've had one hell of a day besides. But I think—I think I can make all of this trouble worthwhile."

She stood, waves of vital signs dancing behind her head.

She held out her hand.

"Join me."

"What?"

"Join me, Eliza," Viktoriya repeated. "Help me help people like us. We can change the world, this terrible, awful world. We can make it safe, for the immuno-compromised, and then for everyone." She chuckled. "It's not like we won't have time. Oh, time—*time!*—that ephemeral thing, that inconstant constant that's hounded us for our entire lives, our entire sicknesses, that drove us, willingly—or so we believed—to transplantation, that forced us to agree. To become cogs in a system that we knew—we *knew*—was broken. That wasn't built for *us*. Time, that forced us into a stagnant world of medical care, into post-transplant treatments that haven't been updated in decades, onto the sidelines as miraculous advances keep passing us by. Time, that cruel mistress, that wretched bitch, that forced us to trade one disease for another. Because we thought we had to. Because we though there was no other alternative. Because that was the only way to get more *time*!

"Together, Eliza, you and I, we can overthrow the shackles of society, of omnipresent, normalized, systemic ableism, and rule the galaxy! And, yes, all right, probably not that last part—interstellar travel is so far down my list—I'm just very excited—but you understand what I am saying, don't you?" Vik thrust her outstretched hand closer, the appendage practically vibrating. "Don't you? Oh, please say you do, Eliza."

Eliza, eyes locked on her friend, didn't reach out, didn't take Viktoriya's hand—but she didn't get up and run either. Even seeing everything she'd seen, hearing everything she'd heard, the stories, the atrocities, the blood and the bones and the bodies—even after all of that, hesitancy paralyzed her. Disbelief, certainly, denial, but devotion, too.

She had already lost so much, hadn't she? So many friends, anything she felt good calling a life. Could she really handle losing Viktoriya on top of it? Her one and only companion, the singular stalwart support she had in the world. Eliza wouldn't admit it—and, really, who would she admit it to?—but she'd been a wreck these past few months, worrying. Waiting. Sinking farther and farther into despair, into isolation, into herself and all her worst impulses. And yet, when Vik had messaged her, she'd jumped. Ran out, without thinking, to an island, into a snowstorm, in her sandals, because it was Viktoriya.

Of course, on the *other* hand, Vik *was* a supervillain.

Or was she? Maybe she was more like the guys who built the Six Million Dollar Man? That was a real question, Eliza had never watched the show, had no idea if they were mysterious benefactors or, like, an evil corporation or something. Had no idea if there was a pile of Five Million Dollar Men behind a shed in the backyard somewhere. And they did build a Bionic Woman, too, so how evil could they really be? Although Eliza was pretty sure they didn't also force the rest of the world into being less-than-bionic to get revenge.

But, let's be real, Vik *was* raising some good points, in between all the monologuing and threatening to dissect Eliza. People *did* suck. Society definitely needed to learn at least a couple lessons. And getting to live forever? That seemed like an opportunity worth at least *considering*. That whole spiel about time was absolutely right; she'd seen plenty of other people in her condition, via lurking in various Facebooks groups, completely *consumed* by the need to do *everything* while they could. Plus it's not like Eliza hadn't been dissected once in her life already. A second time might even be *easier*, seeing as how she'd know what to—

There was movement on one of the tables, on the other side of the room, one of the unoperated-on bodies struggling, weakly, beneath the sheet. A gasping mouth breathing cotton instead of air. A hand pushing, pulling, searching, before falling limp again, sliding off the side of the table.

A hand with blue nails, painted with snowmen.

Justina.

"What did you do to her?" Eliza asked, standing suddenly and stepping away from Viktoriya. "*What did you do?*"

"What? Who?" she replied, craning her neck over her shoulder. "Your future former 'booty call?' Is she awake? I haven't done anything to her. Not yet anyway." She turned back to Eliza, smirking and fighting against a laugh. "She's a YouTuber, Eliza. A digital clown in the thrall of an algorithm. She lives her life in the service of more *views*. The world is certainly not going to *miss* her, and think about how much I could learn, training my organs on her! Turning her in patient zero, the first *living* healthy—after they get the mechanics down on all these venture capital corpses—to be forced into a transplant, into immunosuppression. She'd go down in history books." She paused, furrowing her brow. "You don't—do you sincerely think you have feelings for that inflatable sex doll over there?"

"I don't—maybe? She—she was nice to me, and I know that sounds stupid and small, but, honestly, that hasn't happened in a very, very long time and I—well, I'm kinda confused about it, honestly. I don't know how I feel, or what I want, or what we could even—but I'd like the chance. And, Jesus, Vik, *murdering* her seems very wrong. *That* I'm confident about. The douchebuddies, fine, they've proved how hard they suck, but she's—"

"Have you actually seen her videos?" Viktoriya asked. "They're ninety-five percent cleavage, Eliza. I'm sure she's helping *someone* to sleep, but certainly not in the Little Miss Wholesome way she's pretending."

"Okay, well, now you're just slut-shaming. And even if that *is* what's happening—and I'm not sure ninety-five percent cleavage is even *possible* on YouTube with all the robot censors—there's no reason to—"

The sound of rending metal screamed through the laboratory. Shoulders instinctively rising, faces scrunching from the noise, Eliza and Viktoriya turned. The door to the alchemy workshop-cum-storage closet was denting, outward, as if from an enormous fist on the other side.

"Use the fucking handle!" Eliza shouted over the pounding, screaking din.

There was a pause, and then the door, quietly, swung open. A towering juggernaut of internal organs, a squirming pile of hearts and lungs and stomachs and colons and spinal cords, tongues and tonsils and testicles, covered in patches of taut, triangular stretches of skin, the creature larger even than the offal-ogre from earlier, began squeezing awkwardly through the frame, organs sliding back or falling off to fit through the space.

Then, after reconstituting themselves again: "Viktoriya Hong!" the juggernaut shouted. There was no mouth, not even a makeshift one. The words came from somewhere inside, from every part of the creature all at once. "The time for your reckoning is at hand!"

"Oh, shit, right," Eliza said, turning back to Viktoriya. "So, uh, any chance you could maybe turn all those organs back into dumb meat again? Or has that ship sailed?"

"Turn them back? I am quite honestly shocked, Eliza. To *remove* the gift of consciousness is a crime worse than death. To willingly send a creature, a being of thought, even one so primordial as this, into an abyss of—"

"Right, sure, fine." She turned to the juggernaut. "Sorry, organs! I tried!"

"Then the die has been cast," the organs replied in that ancient and eldritch and impeded voice. "We will keep no terms with our enemies. We are, by your hand, miserable, and you shall share our wretchedness. Let us try our strength in a fight, a final battle in which one must fall.

"The one, in this case, being you, Viktoriya, perchance that was not clear."

"I had hoped it wouldn't come to this," Viktoriya replied, pouting her lips performatively. "That maybe you could still be of *some* service to me, but, if this is what you want ..." She whistled again, three times, sharp and shrill. "To me, my babies!" she called out. "Protect Mommy from your evil forebears! From this monster of mistakes and bad science!"

The organs—*her* organs—rushed in from the other room, hundreds of them, charging like a pack of dogs, and, stopping between Viktoriya and the other organ-beast, began coming together into their own juggernaut. Gallbladders and pancreases climbed atop one another, stacking themselves into a thin, pipe-cleaner armature. Spinal cords and nerve bundles began wrapping around.

The next layer, however, was more hesitant, less certain, as organs bumped into other organs or fell off, the actual *building* happening slowly and haphazardly— and a little too much of both for Viktoriya's tastes.

"No, not there, hearts," she shouted, approaching and waving her arms, "you need to go inside—*inside*— you're *hearts* for Christ's sake! You beat and give strength to everything else! You should know that!

"Please," she said to the other organs, "if you could give us a moment."

"Oh, uh ... of course," the juggernaut said, "that would only be sporting." Meanwhile, their organs were shifting and reconfiguring, obviously learning something from Viktoriya's more structurally-sound construction efforts.

Eliza watched Viktoriya, screeching at her would-be colossus like a fed-up foreman at a team of drunken donkeys, pointing and occasionally shoving the organs into place. Was that what Eliza's future held? Offal-ogres and shouting? Manic episodes of megalomania? Always going, always clawing for more, more, more?

It seemed like a lot of effort.

Because, truthfully, as much as she complained, as much as she fought against the notion, Eliza was actually getting used to her life as a freelance drug dealer. She was even kind of *enjoying* it. For one thing, pot was great. She hadn't had an anxiety attack in months. Even her doctors seemed okay with it, in a *don't ask, don't tell* kind of way, but, still. She set her own hours, worked when she wanted to work. Met infinitely more interesting people than when she was at Forrester FutureTech. And, far from what Hollywood would have you believe, peddling cannabis wasn't actually all that scary or stressful, even in South Carolina. People were *happy* when she rolled up. Life was quiet, easy, maybe even peaceful.

It certainly wasn't the life Eliza had had, or the life she'd expected, or even particularly wanted, but it *was* hers. To do with as she did or didn't please. And wasn't that what she—and me and you and everyone—always *really* wanted? What had being too smart ever gotten Eliza? Stressing over assignments until she made herself sick? Until she made her actual sickness that much worse? A made-up dead-end job in an industry built to be tumultuous, one where she'd always end up owing her entire career to the slightest whim of some idiot tech-bro fucknozzle? Nearly getting killed—several times—by deranged, mutant, killer, monster organs? Because she, once upon a fucking time, coaxed silver nitrate into a vague bridge shape?

Sure, Eliza always said she wanted to be an action movie hero, wanted to punch a German and save the girl, but, shit, even John McClane took a day off every once in a while. "Not wanting to be there" was pretty much his entire arc. Adventure was only fun if it *ended*, if you had somewhere to go after.

And doing all of that *forever*? Fuck off. She could barely handle *right now*.

As the third act of a Marvel movie thundered behind her—as one enormous, always-slithering meat-monster punched another enormous, always -slithering meat-monster, as organs flew through the air and crawled back to where they were—Eliza slid from her stool and poured her half-finished LaCroix onto the nearest, most-important-looking console, carbonated water fizzing and seeping into the circuits. Righteous vengeance was fun and all and, even now, Eliza had no moral qualms with the prospect, but *nobody* needed what was going on in this lab.

With sparks beginning to fly and screens starting to blink, with Viktoriya otherwise involved, Eliza made a break for Justina, the ASMRtist stirring once again into consciousness atop her table. Clement, dead-eyed and still standing there, didn't stop her, or even seem to register that anything of any import was happening.

"Sorry, bud," Eliza mumbled, patting him on the shoulder.

Running—well, limping, really—in a half-crouch across the laboratory, just in case someone or something cared, Eliza settled beside the operating table and pulled back the sheet. Justina Moore looked as perfect as ever, groggy, but no visible injuries or surgeries. Her skirt and ruffled top a little worse for wear, artfully distressed somehow, but nothing that would hinder fleeing into a snowstorm.

"Hey," Justina slurred, her eyes dreamy from sedatives.

"Hi. Can you walk? 'cause we really need to run."

"Yeah," she mumbled, struggling to sitting, "okay."

Arms draped over each other's shoulders, the women made their way to the other half of the lab, away from the monsters and the mad scientist. Eliza had seen an old-ass door near the stills earlier, half-blocked and painted over, clearly forgotten, and had an inkling it was the end result of some kind of smuggling route. Yoinking some equally old-ass keys off the wall, she unlocked the door, wrenched it open, banging against shelving in the process. Then she shoved Justina inside.

"Oh, it's dark in here," the YouTuber mumbled. "Where'd you go? Do you have my phone? Or a … a thing, the clicky-click stick that makes light? I forget what it's called. I don't have my phone."

Neither did Eliza; she'd left it in her bag. She grabbed a portable burner from the shelf, a couple of butane canisters, and turned it on, the small blue flame hissing to life. The tunnel not exactly illuminated, but significantly less impossibly dark.

Hanging back for a moment, one shredded sandal in the tunnel and one in the lab, Eliza watched Viktoriya Hong, her friend and confidante, coaching a colossus she'd constructed from sentient, brainwashed, internal organs through a fistfight with another one.

"Your left!" she was shouting, punching the air. "Your other left!"

"Vik, come on," Eliza called. She'd give her one last chance. She owed her that much. "Vik, leave this, let it go. We need to get out of here. There is absolutely no way this ends well."

Justina, reaching past Eliza and fumbling for her own burner, managed to grab one long enough to turn it one, and then almost immediately dropped it. The flickering flame caught the edge of some stray papers, themselves piled under boards of old wood, which were, in turn, behind and beneath the shelves containing all the extra gas canisters.

"Whoops," Justina murmured.

"See? This is what I was talking about."

"Don't be so naïve," Viktoriya shouted back, her eyes wide and wild, "so foolish!" She turned back to the combatting colossi, speaking loudly but calmly over her shoulder. "There's always a way fix something, Eliza, to answer every question and solve every problem."

"Your house is *on fire*."

"That was me," Justina squeaked. "My bad."

"Who cares?" Viktoriya shouted, raising her hands in triumph. "Who cares?! I have created life! Life! And it is on display, here and now, in all its monumental glory! How are you not fascinated, Eliza?"

"You've created murder-meat, Vik, there's a difference."

"That's nothing marketing can't fix." Brooks shot up atop his operating table in the first lab, springing to sitting like a jack-in-the-box. Neat stitches crossed his chest, the souvenir of a perfect clamshell incision. A perfect lung transplant. "I'm with the doctor," he said. "We could probably sell murder-meat to the WWE, or as a strength-based competition show to some kind of reality television producer."

"What in the fucking—"

"It's worked!" Viktoriya shouted, turning to goggle at the reanimated douchebuddy, at the garbagest of humans Eliza herself had witnessed choking to death on a pancreas hours earlier. "I've done it!" she repeated, falling to her knees. "I am a *god*!"

INFERNAL ORGANS

Beside Eliza, the wooden boards, old shelving or a drawbar for the door, finally caught, orange flames licking and crawling beneath pluming smoke. She looked once more to Viktoriya, to the thundering juggernauts, the living organs being smashed and splattered, to the little marketing shit who Vik hadn't just saved, but brought back from the actual dead.

Then, a tugging on her arm, she ducked into the tunnel.

THE SNOWSTORM WAS, TECHNICALLY, ABATING, lessening in ferocity as dawn approached and various meteorological factors shifted. But that knowledge, had Eliza and Justina had access to such a thing, would have been of little comfort and of even less consequence. As far as the women were concerned—the two of them wildly underdressed for such a weather event, in a Baja pullover and a sporty fall coat, respectively, articles that were warmer than nothing, but not by much—the two of them trudging, side-by-side, through four inches of crusted snowfall, through wind that chapped their faces and pelted them with ice, through walls of blowing whiteness that cut off their vision—the weather was and would remain a terrible blizzard sent straight from Hell to punish them for crimes unknown.

The smuggler's tunnel had led not to freedom, as

Eliza had hoped, had not been a quick and dry escape route straight to the shore, but, rather, an underground entry to the servants' quarters, to one more dusty and ancient section of Grimke Manor's storied—and most likely unseemly, despite Viktoriya's assertions otherwise—past. The quarters were, also, conveniently enough, where Justina and Eliza's belongings were being kept, her hoodie and messenger bag, thrown into a heap with all the douchebuddies' wallets and a not inconsequential amount of gold. This, naturally, raised a lot of questions about Viktoriya's actual intentions toward Eliza, but also helped to alleviate any doubts that she'd done the right thing leaving Vik behind.

It'd also made Eliza about two hundred dollars richer, and possibly more, if the thumb drives she found were indeed crypto keys, and if she could figure out what crypto actually was and how to do it. She'd thought about grabbing the gold, too, but there was only so much a person could fit into a messenger bag. And if *Futurama* had taught her anything, it's that solid gold was not conducive to a quick escape.

"Where are we going?" Justina shouted.

"The dock?" Eliza shouted back. "Carol and Alf's boat should be there—maybe?—assuming it's still in one piece or hasn't blown away or whatever. If it isn't, I think I saw a boathouse over by the lighthouse."

"There's a lighthouse?"

She pointed. "It's that blurry, bright spot over there."

"Are you sure? 'cause that doesn't look like a lighthouse to me."

"Yeah, me either."

They trudged on, hand-in-hand, twin ghosts amongst the blowing snow. Behind them, Grimke Manor creaked and popped, flames beginning to lap from the windows, from the upper floors. Smoke rising in thick, black sheets, twisting in the wind, disappearing into the storm.

Then, seeing the large, dark shadows of the island's gargantuan live oaks shimmer into view ahead, the women hurried forward, running, stumbling, as quick as they were able, and entering into the corridor of trees. The wide, interlocking branches and massive trunks formed a temporary and much-needed break from the worst of the wind and snow.

"Thank crap," Justina said, shivering, her arms clenched tightly across her midsection, hands tucked into her armpits. "You think we could start a fire here? I mean, I'm assuming you have a lighter. No offense intended, if that's, like, rude. It's just, the drug rug and your general vibe and everything."

"No, you're right," Eliza said, patting the bag hanging at her hip. "Maybe we can set up some kind of camp until—"

There was a loud crack, in the branches above them, the sound scarcely audible over the storm. But loud enough. Eliza looked up, toward the quivering end of a snapped branch. Something was moving along the tangled web of ice and tree. Something darting, sidewinding, in a way the wind, no matter how fierce, could never.

Something long and pink and carrying a crowbar.

Something very much like that goddamn large intestine.

"Son of a—"

Before Eliza could finish swearing, the intestine jumped, fell, crashing against the ground at her feet, the crowbar clattering against the snow-dusted cobble-stone—and nearly clobbering Eliza in the process.

This time, though, she was ready.

INFERNAL ORGANS

As the large intestine coiled, preparing to lunge again, Eliza kicked out a battered sandal, kicked up like a soccer player, catching the flesh of the organ with her heel, and the crowbar with her bare toes. Something crunched and almost certainly broke in the process, but Eliza's feet were so frozen, she couldn't feel anything. The weapon skipped down the path.

The cecum, the wide, rounded pouch at the head of the intestine, lifted and spread wider. The attached appendix, a thin tube like a grotesque gummi worm, hanging limp from the cecum, began fluttering and hissing, the whole thing looking like a cobra about to strike.

But Eliza was faster. Angrier. She grabbed the intestinal tract by what would have been the throat if the intestine had actually been a snake, but what was, in fact, just more intestine. She held it, staring into the wet, pink skin that would have been its eyes.

No hospital scene was reflected back at her. No visions of her own anguish, no suffering, no years-old trauma, manifested. No memories rose up like mountains, burying her, stealing her away from the present; no fear of death crept through the dark and crippled her. The image of herself, thin and malnourished, maniacally laughing as she sat on a hospital toilet, shitting blood and water, the acrid sting of bleach and antibiotics filling her nostrils, the panic and fury and absurdity of going out like *this*, of dying on a hospital toilet, was nowhere to be found.

Instead, in her hands, all she saw was an asshole with a crowbar.

"What the fuck is your problem, intestine?!"

Digging her fingers into the pink flesh, Eliza pulled and pulled, tearing the intestine into two distinct, and distinctly unmoving, pieces. Something warm spattered against Eliza, against her chest, her face. She very quickly made the decision not to think about it. Instead, she dropped the organ to the ground and began jumping, stamping, until the intestine was nothing but a stain against the cobblestone.

"Did you and that giant worm have a history?" Justina asked.

"It was an intestine, and, yeah, kind of," Eliza answered. "I don't really want to talk about it."

"Sounds good to me."

And so they continued on, under the trees and back into the storm.

+++++++++

By the time Eliza and Justina stumbled onto the dock, the snow had eased enough that they could see, clearly, for ten feet in front of them. Could make out shapes and colors beyond that. All of which unfortunately meant that the lack of their longed-for watercraft, the missing McClanahan boat, wasn't simply a trick of the eye.

"Fuck."

"I'm so tired," Justina muttered. "And cold. How far is the lighthouse?"

"Far," Eliza answered. "And there's rocks."

"Fuuuck."

"Pretty much, yeah."

As Eliza considered slogging back to the relative shelter of the oak trees, starting a fire, and contending with whatever rusty tool-wielding organs fell on her as they happened—as Justina stared at the inferno of Grimke Manor, tried to locate the neighboring servants' quarters, and wondered just how much smoke inhalation was *too much* smoke inhalation—they both heard the thrumming roar of an engine in the distance, across the inlet. A sound that got closer and closer and closer, until, eventually, until it revealed itself to be a boat. Until it revealed itself to be Walton Goggins piloting a rickety lobster boat, like *The Orca* from *Jaws*.

"Walton?" Eliza asked, the engine thinning. The boat settled softly along the foot of the dock.

"Walter," he corrected from his perch atop the main cabin. "Goggles." He had dark bruises across the left side of his face and neck, accompanied by dozens of small, red cuts all over, the kind one might receive if, hypothetically, they were thrown through a plate-glass window by an ogre made of reanimated offal. "But I look enough like the real guy, and I'm not against leaning in sometimes, pretending to be interested in investing in some rich nutcase's pie-in-the-sky *whatever* and getting a nice weekend out of it. Then the *real* Walton's stuck telling them no. It's not a bad life.

"Usually anyway."

Eliza stepped onto the boat, stumbling and holding Justina for support.

"And you know how to drive—pilot?—sail?—a boat?" she asked.

"I mean, I'm here, aren't I?" The engine roared back to life again. Walter Goggles cut the helm sharply, taking the boat out. "I'd like to see the real Walton do that."

+++++++++

Buried in blankets and towels and life vests, Justina and Eliza sat huddled together on a benchseat inside the cabin, a portable heater pulled close. Their clothes, soaked through with snow, were draped across every flat surface. Through the windows, the storm was, finally, receding, the blowing snow reduced to a few fleeting flurries. The first rays of sunrise were throwing warm light over everything.

"... actually got a doctorate in Shakespearean literature," Justina was saying. "But it turns out whispering treacly affirmations to strangers on the internet is *a lot* more profitable than getting kids to give a shit about the nuances of historical drama."

"But why keep up the charade?" Eliza asked. "When you're not online?"

"Brand integrity? Or, if you mean last night specifically, because I thought maybe this was some kind of Mr. Beast prank."

"I don't know who that is."

"He's an internet celebrity, always pulling over-the-top shit like this when he could just be funding food banks and buying houses for poor people while keeping his mouth shut, instead of turning everything into some self-aggrandizing public-relations stunt. That's why I was here, actually, what I was trying to do, put some of my money into advancing the post-transplant process. You know they haven't updated that shit since the '80s?"

"I know," Eliza said. "How'd you get into it? The ASMRing?"

"I saw and opportunity and grabbed it, I guess? I was making videos for class, back when I was still teaching, reading soliloquies and stuff, acting and using different accents and shit, putting them online. And, I don't know, people—not my students, obviously—really responded. The friend who'd been helping me, an AV guy, turned me on to the whole ASMR thing. Everything kind of snowballed from there."

Eliza smiled, small. "I think I need to learn how to do that. Grab opportunities. Not spend years and years talking myself into something, and then five seconds getting back out of it."

"Well, my shithead middle-graders notwithstanding, I *am* a pretty good teacher." Justina bumped her shoulder against Eliza's. "So," she continued, "what're you doing for Christmas? My friends and I are having a bonfire down at Folly Beach on the twenty-fourth if you're going to be around ..."

The women leaned closer together, skin against skin, fingers tangling, feeling each other's flushing warmth, each other's rushing pulse. The thrill and contentment of two hearts beating as one.

And, beneath the benchseat, in Eliza's bag, a third heart.

Not beating.

Not yet.

about the author

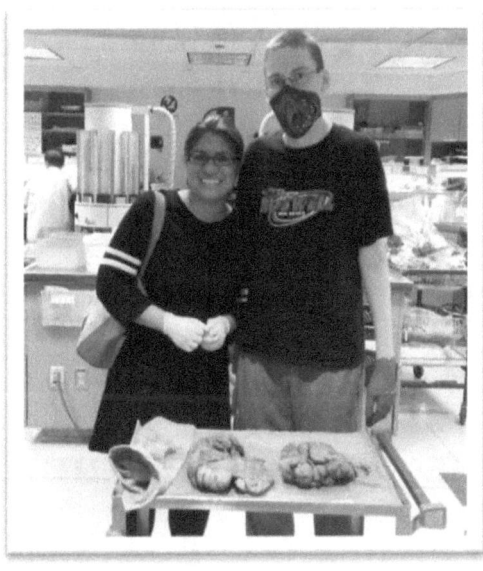

EIRIK GUMENY is the editor of Atomic Carnival Books and author of *Beggars Would Ride; The Greatest Gatsby: an American Werewolf in West Egg;* and the *Exponential Apocalypse* series. His short fiction has appeared in, among others, *Impossible Worlds*, *Kaleidotrope*, *Soul Jar* (Forest Avenue Press), and *Escalators to Hell* (From Beyond Press). His nonfiction has been published by *Cracked*, *Wired*, and *The New York Times*.

In 2014, he received a double lung transplant and technically died a little. He got better.

Find him at EGumeny.com or on Bluesky.

also by the author

THE
EXPONENTIAL APOCALYPSE
SERIES

Exponential Apocalypse
Dead Presidents
High Voltage
Revenge-aroni
Black Hole, Son!
The End of Everything Forever

BEGGARS WOULD RIDE

THE GREATEST GATSBY,
or, an American Werewolf in West Egg

QUINTOLOGY OF QUALMS

WE'RE GOING TO DIE HERE,
AREN'T WE?

DEVIL WENT DOWN TO JERSEY

also from
ATOMIC CARNIVAL
BOOKS

OPEN ALL NIGHT
an anthology of retail horror

GREATER THAN HIS NATURE
thrilling tales of mad science

EAT THE RICH
an anthology of carnivorous anti-capitalism